Nancy Welch
6220 Montalcino Dr.
Round Rock, Texas 78665

(813) 205-5130

Return to Cape

San Blas

A Novel

NANCY WELCH

WESTBOW
P R E S S°
A DIVISION OF THOMAS NELSON
& ZONDERVAN

Scriptures taken from the Holy Bible, New International Version®, NIV®. Copyright © 1973, 1978, 1984, 2011 by Biblica, Inc.™ Used by permission of Zondervan. All rights reserved worldwide. www.zondervan.com The "NIV" and "New International Version" are trademarks registered in the United States Patent and Trademark Office by Biblica, Inc.™

Song lyrics of *For Such a Time as This* and related story used with permission from songwriter Wayne Watson.

WestBow Press books may be ordered through booksellers or by contacting:

WestBow Press
A Division of Thomas Nelson & Zondervan
1663 Liberty Drive
Bloomington, IN 47403
www.westbowpress.com
1 (866) 928-1240

Because of the dynamic nature of the Internet, any web addresses or links contained in this book may have changed since publication and may no longer be valid. The views expressed in this work are solely those of the author and do not necessarily reflect the views of the publisher, and the publisher hereby disclaims any responsibility for them.

ISBN: 978-1-9736-5204-5 (sc)
ISBN: 978-1-9736-5205-2 (hc)
ISBN: 978-1-9736-5203-8 (e)

Library of Congress Control Number: 2019900736

Print information available on the last page.

WestBow Press rev. date: 2/27/2019

Dedicated

to

God, my Father, His Son, and Holy Spirit,
who has directed and made possible
every word in this book.

To God be the glory.

and to

my daughter Kimberly,
for without her, there would be no book.
I love her now and forever.

Acknowledgments

To my niece, Dr. Karen Fields, for reading my manuscript, reviewing my daughter's cancer journey that actually began in Pennsylvania, and helping with cancer facts for a new character in this story.

To my friend, Lee, for being an inspiration for an adventuresome character in this story. May she one day learn who murdered the assistant lighthouse keeper in 1938.

To Reverend Dave Landers for being an inspiration for the pastor of the small country church in this story.

To Anthony Sanchez for his ongoing encouragement to write this book, and for his dedication to writing the screenplay.

To Carol Touchton for sharing her dream with me and allowing me to share mine with her.

To Robyn Sitmer for being the first to read my manuscript and give me feedback.

To Shirley Westrate for reading my manuscript and lending me her editing eye.

To Anne Mitru for her friendship and encouragement to make this dream a reality.

To all other friends, too many to name, who have read my manuscript and been an encouragement.

To my two sons for their belief in my writing and inspiration.

This is the place where God's hand
touches the earth.

Kimberly Michelle Welch Michael (1971-2003)

One

I can still hear the sound of that old screen door as it slammed gently against the worn wooden doorframe when I would come home from school. "Ma, I'm home," I would call out as I made my way to the back of our house to wherever my mother would be busying herself with household chores. Ma was the personification of Auntie Em on *The Wizard of OZ.* Sometimes, she would be out back, hanging the clothes on the line. Sometimes, she was ironing in the bedroom, the steam coming up from the ironing board as she pressed the collar on my dad's shirt. And many times, I'd find her in the kitchen with her apron on, flour on her hands and dusted across her cheek, leaning over that old rusted recipe box as she prepared dinner.

This is what I would remember when I travelled back home to the Cape. As I gazed out the large picture window of the Greyhound bus, the miles and miles of St. Joe Paper Company trees going by in a blur, I thought how strange it was that I should be returning home now, at such a time as this.

The recent words of my doctor reverberated in my ear... "You have six months or less to live. Your cancer is aggressive, probably two, or three, or four months." Just like that! One minute I had a life… filled with the busyness of being a young woman, just twenty-nine, working in corporate America in downtown Tampa and the single parent of my almost two-year-old daughter Briana. The next, it was as if my life was suspended… only it wasn't suspended. The clock was ticking, and I had to make plans, plans for my little girl.

The bus ride back to the Cape was long and slow. I was weary from the trip, my little daughter sleeping across the seat, her head in my lap. Little did she know how much her life was about to change. Little did she know that she was about to lose her mother.

I wasn't initially told that my cancer was terminal. One evening when I was in bed, I found a lump in my breast. I followed up with my doctor and had a biopsy. I was only twenty-eight years old, and mammograms weren't recommended until women reached the age of thirty-five. I called my mother the night before I got the results of the biopsy.

"Kristen, don't worry," she said. "You are young and look vibrantly healthy. The chances of it being cancer at your age are low."

The next day, I got the results – it *was* cancer.

Little did I know at the time that my cancer had been misdiagnosed as breast cancer. My mother wanted to come, but I pleaded with her not to. I was scheduled for surgery, a lumpectomy, and underwent radiation and brutal chemotherapy treatments. With the help of my friends and colleagues at work, I managed to get through it. Then, supposedly, I was fine… a survivor of breast cancer.

About five months later, I experienced excruciating pain in my back. I had broken down and cried in pain on the phone to my mother. "My doctor is sending me to a pain management specialist," I told her.

"Kristen, you don't need a pain management specialist," she said emphatically. "You need to know what is causing the pain. The pain is just a symptom, and your doctor needs to find out what is causing it!"

At her insistence, I pushed to find answers. Further testing would reveal the diagnosis no one ever wants to hear.

It was the morning of 9/11 – *September 11, 2001* – when I would learn the truth. I had to call Terry, the corporate attorney I worked for, and let her know that I would be in late after a doctor's appointment. As I dialed the number, uneasiness engulfed my body. I felt this would be a significant day, kind of like the feeling one gets in the calm just before a storm. I felt as if my life was about to change.

"Terry, hi, it's Kristen," I said. "I have a doctor's appointment this morning to get the results of testing regarding that pain I've been having in my back. I shouldn't be in to work too late."

Terry responded as I thought she would, "Take all the time you need, and good luck."

Actually, I lucked out when I got hired to be Terry Matheson's paralegal in a large law firm in Tampa. Not only was she a great boss to work for, she was a great mentor. When I left Cape San Blas almost three years ago, I had been attending law school in Tallahassee. When I left the Cape, I left those hopes and dreams behind. One day, though, I would finish my education and be where Terry is. I envisioned being colleagues and working within the same law firm. At least that's what I told myself. That was the new plan.

Although I had made an early morning appointment, the doctor's office was full when I arrived. I took my seat among other patients who were reading magazines as if they didn't have a care in the world or any other place they had to be. I was amazed when I was called after only being seated for about seven minutes. I know now that it was probably because of their discovery and my prognosis. The nurses were probably waiting for the news to be delivered to me, news that they had known for no telling how long.

The door to the back treatment area opened, and a young nurse appeared. "Number 15," she announced with a raised voice.

I, along with my fellow patient comrades, had been reduced to a number to protect our privacy. As I stood up from my seat and strolled across the room, I wondered how this could possibly protect my privacy. All eyes were on me.

Once we were back in the treatment room, my young nurse turned to me and reported that Dr. Rollins would be with me momentarily. No how are you. No step up on the scale and let's weigh you. Her job on this fateful day had just been to escort me back to a treatment room and close the door.

Dr. Rollins appeared as his nurse had said – momentarily. "Miss Parker..."

Thank the Lord, I have a name now, I thought. "Did anyone come with you today?" he asked. Did anyone come with me? What kind of question was that?

"No, Dr. Rollins. Why?"

"I have the results of your tests back. Miss Parker, your cancer was not breast cancer as we had originally thought. It's a rare cancer called small cell cancer and is now in your spine. We had the pathologist compare the original slides. This kind of cancer doesn't usually start in your breast... it starts in your lungs. Now, it's in your lungs and spine. That is why you have been having the back pain."

"Back pain," he had said. To refer to what I have been experiencing as simply "back pain" was an understatement. What I had been experiencing was excruciating, severe, almost torture.

"Small cell cancer? What is the next step?" I asked Dr. Rollins. "What do we do now?"

Dr. Rollins looked down at my file and paused. "Small cell cancer is aggressive," he said. "You have six months or less to live, probably two, or three, or four months."

"But, Dr. Rollins, I have plans... plans to finish my education, plans for my future, plans for my little girl."

"I'm sorry," Dr. Rollins said as he again looked down at my file.

I wanted to run out of the room, run from all the words this doctor had just uttered. I didn't have time now to stop and pay the bill or check out. I needed to find a place where they could cure my cancer. I needed to live my life. I needed to take care of my little girl.

Somehow, I made it through downtown Tampa traffic in my leased Volvo coupe back to Matheson, Masters & Klein. Tension seemed to fill the air. As I stepped off the elevator and made my way down the hall, I noticed employees in different departments gathered around television sets. What they were watching couldn't be more important than the news that had just been delivered in my doctor's office. I spotted Terry.

"Terry," I blurted out. "I need to talk with you."

"Kristen," she interrupted, "have you been watching the news? One of the Twin Towers has just been hit by terrorists."

I turned as if in slow motion and glanced at a TV. Just then, a plane crashed into a second Twin Tower and it came tumbling down. Ashes and ruble engulfed the street and headed straight for the television screen. What was happening on this 9/11? Our security as a nation was being threatened. Would we ever be the same? Would I ever be the same after this day?

These were the thoughts that were etched in my mind as I made my way back to my childhood home on the Cape. The brakes gave way to the sound of resistance against the pavement, and the bus came to a slow stop. Not a passenger moved; only the stirring sounds of people shifting in their seats to see why the bus had stopped and slowly waking children asking, "Where are we?" The bus driver opened the door, descended the steps, and began busying himself with the task of opening the outside luggage compartment to retrieve whatever belonged to the lucky passenger who was getting off at this stop. I glanced out the window and recognized the "T" intersection – we were on two-lane State Road 30 with the vast expanse of sandy peninsula road 30-E going off to the left. We were at the Cape. *We were home.*

Two

As I travel the beaten path, the Greyhound bus pulling away behind me, I can feel the miles and miles of sand dunes and wide-open sky on the Cape beckoning me. I feel like I am coming back home to God, away from the noises of my life, away from the chattering of my thoughts about work each day, or assignments that are due, or chores that need to be done. Have I forgotten how close I feel to God here? My pace picks up, suitcase in one hand and my little Briana in the other. My excitement seems to bubble over into my beautiful little daughter. She doesn't know why my heart leaps, but she begins to be filled with excitement as well.

How long it has been since I have been here. I left the Cape and ran away to have a life… and lost it. I ran away from evil done to me… but also from those I love. I ran away from the place where I feel most alive in the world. How could I have forgotten? The sun shines through the thin pine trees that line the path. The sand beneath my feet seems to beckon to me as I begin to hurry along, my anticipation growing stronger with each step. The sound of the ocean grows closer.

Then I see her… Mom is coming down the front porch steps, the screen door slowly finding its way back to the old frame house. "Ma" had become "Mom," a term of endearment, in my early twenties. As I got older, my mother seemed to get younger and wiser. Maybe it was just the times. Maybe it was because I was growing up. She became my best friend. How could I have left the Cape and not confided in her?

"Mom!" I call as I begin to pick up my step to run to her as best I can with little Briana in tow. "Mom!"

As we reach one another midway, our arms intertwine, Briana giggling at our side. "Mom, I am so glad to be home," I cry. Inside, my heart is screaming, "Oh Mom, I'm dying!"

As we release our embrace, Mom looks down and takes Briana's hand. "And who might this be?" she knowingly asks.

Another giggle, and Briana responds with a very matter of fact tone, "Briana."

Mom gathers her up in her arms as I take our suitcase and we head in the direction of home.

I follow Mom back to my old bedroom where she has made a little bed for Briana from a small crib-size toddler bed she picked up in Apalachicola at a yard sale. The worn curtains at the southwest window gently blow in and I feel the soft warm breeze. How different from my leased condo in Tampa with windows shut tightly and locked and constant air conditioning. I take a deep breath and smell the sea air. The *Forgotten Coast…* how I had wished in Tampa I could have forgotten it.

"Are you girls hungry?" Mom asks. It was getting quite late past lunch.

"Yes," I answer. "Briana, are you hungry?"

Mom interrupts with, "I thought we'd have good ole Campbell's tomato soup and grilled cheese sandwiches."

"Perfect! Briana loves grilled cheese and you know tomato soup is one of my favorites."

Briana claps her hands.

As we sit at the table in our old eat-in kitchen, the back door open with just the screen door closed, I feel as though I'm a teenager again, back home having lunch with my mother.

"Where's Lucky?" I ask. Lucky is our black lab who is usually not far from the house and stretched out sleeping.

"Your brother Jacob took him with him down to the fish house to get some oysters and shrimp for tonight. I thought we'd have an oyster roast later."

"Isn't Jacob too young for a learner's permit?"

"You know he is, Kristen, but if he just goes the back roads from the Cape to the fish house in Apalachicola, no one cares. Just like you, you started driving on the Cape and to and from Apalachicola when you were about his age."

An oyster roast! I remember the many evenings Dad would build a big bonfire in the backyard, and we'd roast oysters in their shell right in the coals. Dad would always get shrimp for Mom because she didn't like oysters. Mom would take the top of the broiler pan, put it down on some coals, brush her shrimp with lemon juice and butter, and they'd be done in five minutes. I was an oyster girl and had been since I was about two-years-old. Briana had never seen a bonfire. In Tampa, it would be against a city or county ordinance to do such a thing, even if you could find a place to have one.

Ah, the time of oyster roasts! That was back in the day when Dad used to spend time with the family, my mother, two younger brothers, and me. Dad would call me "Princess" and let me tag along with him. My dad was a man of the sea and made his living mostly from oysterin'. He could usually be found in the bay waters of St. Vincent Sound at the patch of Sheephead Bayou. You couldn't tell where Dad left off and the Bay began. St. Vincent Sound is just east of the Cape and southwest of Apalachicola, an oysterman's haven.

In 1985, when the oyster harvesting slowed, Dad began to go crazy. My mother said it was midlife crisis. Dad, after all, was thirty-five at the time. He started withdrawing from us, the very ones who loved him, and became preoccupied with his "projects." I was fourteen years old, a time in my life when I needed my dad most.

When the oyster harvesting slowed, the means by which Dad defined his purpose in life diminished. Maybe it was his lack of producing an oyster harvest to be proud of that made him feel inadequate and withdraw from us. Didn't he know that all we needed was him? Didn't he know that he was more than the massive pounds of oysters he harvested every year? No, he didn't.

Shrimp had increased in value during that time, but oysterin' had been Dad's main harvest, and the sheer enormity of his harvest had given him great satisfaction. Sometimes Dad would do some sport fishing charters when it suited him or to make money for Christmas. But shrimpin'? No, Dad was an oysterman.

I was unpacking my suitcase, slowly putting my clothes away in the old dresser and vanity drawers, when the crushing sound of tires on the oyster shell drive alerted me that someone had just pulled up. Before I made it to the front of our small bungalow, I heard Lucky's bark.

As I made my way down the front porch steps and across to the drive, my oldest brother's 4-wheel-drive pick-up truck pulled up at the same time. Johnny had heard I was back in town and came as soon as he had completed his delivery of seafood to the packing house.

Jacob, my youngest brother, had gone around to the back of the house with his treasure of oysters and shrimp for the roast, so I ran to greet Johnny.

"*Son!*" I called out as I ran to greet him. I had been calling Johnny "*Son*" since he was about ten-years-old and I was his older fifteen-year-old sister.

"Kristen, it's about time you came home!"

As my arms wrapped around him, and his around me, I burrowed my head in the crook of his shoulder and wept for what seemed like eternity.

When I finally pulled back, I pointed to the words on his truck *Parker and Son Seafood and Trucking, Incorporated.* "What's this, *Son?*"

"Oh, Dad helped me start this business, but it's actually mine. A way to make a living."

"*Son's* not going to stay out for days in the hot sun oysterin'," I said, and we both laughed.

Just then, Jacob came from around back and jumped up at both of us. Jacob was almost thirteen and full of spunk. He seemed glad to have both his brother and sister at home for a change. As I hugged him, he teared up, but I tried with all my might not to cry again. Jacob had grown from the tumble-haired boy I remembered and was fast becoming a young man.

"Kristen, when did you start calling Johnny '*Son?*'" Jacob asked. "What's that about?"

"Oh, it started when Johnny was about ten and needed advice from the wise one, me, his older sister, and I would say, 'Now *Son...*' and it just stuck. Hey Jacob, I've got something for you in the house," I said.

"Let's go!" Jacob said as he started leading the way.

"After you," Johnny motioned toward me with an outstretched arm.

As we walked into the house, we had to step over Lucky who was sleeping in the middle of the living room floor under the ceiling fan. I led Jacob and Johnny back to my bedroom and pulled a three-foot long hand-made Christmas stocking from a bag in my suitcase.

"Custom-made and special delivery for one special brother," I said beaming.

I thought Jacob's eyes were going to bug out of his head. He was awestruck. On the stocking were all kinds of hand-made appliqués that were unique for Jacob – a sunny yellow smiley face, representing me smiling at him, a heart with the words "I love you," a star for the star he is, a cross, a Bible, the Holy Spirit that looked like a cross between the gingerbread man and an angel, a white lamb for the Lamb of God and a white dove. There was also a butterfly and fish with the word "Peace" written on it. The large red stocking was hand-sewn with a soft white furry border and his name on the top in glitter writing.

"That's for me? You made that for me?" he asked, slowly pronouncing and emphasizing each word.

"The one and only," I said. "I thought with a stocking this size, maybe you'd get that new fishing pole you've been wanting. When I had to stay home from work in Tampa because the chemotherapy made me so sick, I made it."

Jacob's smile faded, and his facial expression changed to one of puzzlement and sadness. "But Kristen, it isn't Christmas yet. You *will* be here for Christmas, won't you? It's just three months away."

Just then, Briana, who had been taking her nap on the living room sofa, stirred. Saved by the bell... I almost thought I heard it ringing. As I made my way across the room to her, I called back over my shoulder. "I just wanted to give it to you early," I said, "so you can put it out when the time comes."

Dad arrived home about seven and started the fire for the oyster roast. It actually went off without a hitch. He even seemed to be present, mind, body, and spirit, for the whole evening. What a change from having one foot at home and the other foot ready to take off in a running position.

What a long day it had been. I felt as though I never left the Cape ...but I did. I left because I had no choice.

Three

I remember the day I left the Cape as if it was yesterday. It was Monday, January 4th, 1999. My mom, Leigh, Carly, and I were glad to be back together after the New Year's holiday. We were the *Fabulous Four* after all and glad to be up to our old shenanigans.

Carly was my childhood friend. We had been together since the beginning of time. We even looked like sisters. Carly, her full blonde hair falling just below her shoulders, her round cheeks and big blue eyes, was a little more filled out than I. Whenever we played on the beach or she got excited, her cheeks would flush. I had sandy blonde hair too that always fell just below my shoulders, but it fell in soft curls that looked like I'd just paid seventy dollars for an expensive perm. My eyes were blue, too, but sometimes they were green. CarlyAnn, as she was called back then, and I were inseparable. We made sand tea cakes on our pretend kitchen stove made of bricks in the back yard and climbed almost every tree in the area. When we would go down to the City Dock in Apalachicola with Dad, we skated for hours with our old shoe skates, our skate keys hanging around our necks to loosen and tighten them, while we waited for however long it took Dad to dispense of the endless pounds of oysters he had brought in.

Leigh was my mom's friend, but they were more like sisters from another era. She was pixie cute with short hair and eyes that could be playful and mischievous. My mother and I had grown closer as I grew up, and she became my best friend. Mom, Leigh, Carly, and I became the *Fabulous Four*. Mom and I used to tease that we were so much alike that even our friends had the same name – CarlyAnn and Leigh Ann.

Leigh was determined that someday we would become the *Famous Four* when we solved a mystery that was more than sixty years old. In 1938, the assistant lighthouse keeper on the Cape, E. W. Marler, had been murdered. He normally tended the lighthouse in the morning and then spent time in his workshop behind the house. When he didn't show up at home for the noon meal, his wife sent one of his young daughters to fetch him. His daughter found him in a bloodied scene and ran to her mother to report that he was hurt. Mrs. Marler found her husband at the end of his workbench with thirteen stab wounds around his heart, one at his throat, and a hand dangling at his side. The case has never been solved and has fascinated Leigh who is determined that the *Fabulous Four* will uncover what happened.

The day began so promising. Leigh arrived early that morning through the kitchen door to announce that she had discovered an old mansion on one of her walks down the peninsula. She liked to walk as far as she could to discover buried treasures that the tide had deposited on the shore. Carly and I both attended school in Tallahassee and were still off for the Christmas break. I was attending law school and Carly was working toward her degree in marketing. Mom and Leigh worked for the public school system in Franklin County and were also still on break.

"Get your water packed," Leigh said excitedly. "I stumbled across an old mansion way down the peninsula back in the woods. I was too scared to go into it by myself, but today's a perfect day. Let's make a day trip out of it."

"Leigh, are you sure?" Mom asked. "How far down is it? I wouldn't want to get caught in rain."

Just then I walked in, barefoot and still in my bathrobe, hair dripping from the shower. "Hi, Leigh. What's up?"

"Just trying to talk your mom into making a day trip out of hiking down the peninsula to this old mansion I found back in the woods. Are you up for an adventure?"

"Let me check with Carly and see if she has any plans."

With bent head and towel-drying my hair, I made my way across the linoleum floor to the phone at the end of the kitchen counter and dialed Carly's number. There wasn't any answer. Just then, Carly walked in.

"What's up?" she asked as she sat down in a chair at the kitchen table. We all looked at each other, me to Mom, Mom to Leigh, Leigh to me, and then all at Carly. An adventure was in the making.

We packed our water, put on our sun hats and visors, and headed down the peninsula on the shore. Mom packed sandwiches… "just in case," she said. Lucky followed us for a bit but turned back when he saw it was going to be a lengthy expedition.

Our house was on the bay side of the narrow peninsula. We had cut across the path through the dunes and followed that old dune fence, with its thin wooden weathered white paint slats that were held together with wire, to the beach side. The fence was mostly covered by the new sand the sea air had blown in. As we came down the sloping sandy trail, we heard the faint sound of a few seagulls tag-teaming each other as they began to fly over the water.

When we reached the opening and were on the beach, I threw my small duffle down, put my arms straight out and twirled around. The smell of sea air and the miles and miles of sand dunes overtook me. No matter how many times I walked down this shore, I was awestruck by its beauty. Carly joined me, and Leigh and Mom started the trek down the shore, walking slowly so we could catch up. Leigh was anxious to explore the old house she had discovered.

The sky was clear when we started out, not a cloud in sight. We had worn our lightly lined parkas as it was a little cold outside, about 60 degrees. It was, after all, January.

"Leigh, how far down is this place?" Mom asked when we had gone what seemed like almost five miles.

"Not far, I think we're almost there," Leigh responded. By that time, we had all shed our jackets and wrapped them around our waists.

"Good thing," Mom said as she motioned to a graying sky in the distance. "In Florida, you know, rain storms can come up at a moment's notice."

"Hopefully, it will pass by, Mom," I reassured.

We had trekked about another half mile down the shore when Leigh pointed to the right at an opening in the sand dunes with a large piece of driftwood. "There, I think it's there," she said as she led us across the vast sandy beach to a small opening of a trail that led into the woods.

"If I didn't know you'd been here before, I'd say that looked like an animal trail back to their nighttime habitat," Mom said to Leigh. Another time, when we had all been together, we had seen a lone fox trailing along the beach. The Cape was also known for having raccoons, deer, black bear, and even an occasional coyote.

Leigh led the way and pushed a hanging branch back as she entered the trail. "Yep, this is it," she said excitedly as she pushed through with us following her.

The trail went through thin pines and scrub brush. Amazingly, after we got back a ways, the trail was clear and wide enough for us to pass through without having to clear our way. We walked the sandy trail for about ten minutes. Then, we could see bits of an old structure through the trees.

Just then, I felt a raindrop… and then all of a sudden, it began to pour, fast pulsating rain pellets. We all called "Run!" in one fashion or another, and we darted toward the building as if we had lived there all our lives and knew where it was.

Within minutes, we were all standing in a line in front of it… this massive old mansion in the middle of nowhere. We were dumbstruck by the enormity of it at first and just stood there, in the rain, in a straight horizontal line, holding our parkas above our heads.

Then Leigh gave a little chuckle and said, "Shall we?" as she slowly led the way up the very wide front porch steps.

Once up, we all raised our heads as we lowered our parkas and looked around from the left to the right, up at the old ceiling, and back again. Leigh and Mom walked down the old porch to the left and looked around the side of the house. The porch seemed to wrap around it.

Then, they started back across the porch to the right, Carly and I ahead of them, and we looked back around the other side of the house. "The porch does wrap around," I said in confirmation.

We walked back around to the front, slowly and quietly across the old floorboards. I don't know if we thought we were going to wake up the ghosts or if someone might be there.

Leigh quietly opened the front screen door with its ornate wood work in the corners. Cobwebs were everywhere on the porch, in the corners, and hanging from the eaves.

Carly was peering into one of the front windows; then, she looked over at Leigh and said, "It doesn't look like anyone's here. It's rather dark."

So… Leigh turned the knob on the big hardwood front door and it fell open… with a slow scrunching sound.

I couldn't forego the moment and made the sounds, *"Ooh… Ooh… Ooh,"* changing the octaves.

That didn't stop us. We were the *Fabulous Four*, after all. We bravely entered the house as if it were our own.

Everything was dusty and dirty inside the house. There were old long sheet-like drapes at the windows that kept out most of the light. An old fireplace with large mantel greeted us from the wall facing the door. Mom and Leigh went one way toward a large dining room and kitchen and Carly and I went the other into a parlor with beautiful old dusty antique chairs and end tables.

"Oh my," Mom called out, "there's a fireplace in the kitchen!" The old brick fireplace was in the center wall between the dining room and kitchen and opened into both.

Carly and I hurried over and peeked in. The kitchen had lots of windows and a door that also entered onto the wraparound porch. We could see another stairway on the back side of the porch going up to a second floor on the house.

We all went around and up the main stairs in the house by the front door, slowly again at first, and came out on a large landing that had many rooms with many fireplaces. There were no bathrooms and only small cupboard size closets. Everything was dusty. It didn't look like anyone had been in the house, especially on this floor, in a long time.

"Well, let's go back down and have our sandwiches," Mom said. It was still raining outside, although lightly, so it seemed we would be staying for lunch.

"I'll open a window," Carly said as we descended the stairs to the dining room. The window was stuck, and I walked over to help her.

Mom took her place at the end of a long dining room table, the (what used to be) white tablecloth was dark with dust. She set her pack on the table and began to take the sandwiches and chips out.

"Mom, you even brought chips?" Of course, she did. Mom was a planner.

We all sat down, spread our napkins out to lay our sandwiches and chips on, and began eating. We had all brought enough bottled water with us for our daylong trip.

As we sat eating and talking about what the house might have been or who it might have belonged to, Mom seemed focused on an inside wall that was lined with dark built-in cabinets. After a while, she put down her sandwich she had been eating and walked across the room to a tall cabinet door almost big enough to walk through. She slowly opened it.

"Oh my!" she exclaimed when she'd opened the cabinet door.

We all ran over to see what looked like a passageway going off to the left and then around a corner, probably behind the main staircase, I thought.

"Do we dare?" Carly asked.

Leigh got a gleam in her eye and there was that chuckle again. "I'm game," she said. Mom stepped back and let Leigh lead the way.

Although the passageway was mostly dark, there was a shaft of light at the end where it seemed to turn to the right. There must have been something open or a crack in the boards to let the ray of light in. We slowly followed Leigh down the long passageway and around the corner to a small stairway that was just a short distance away.

Leigh looked back but kept trudging on, slowly ascending the stairs in the cramped stairway.

The stairs went to a small landing and then farther on, the total distance seemed like one flight. "Surely, we must be on the second floor," I said, "but I don't remember this from when we were looking around on the second floor."

The short hallway revealed a shut door just down the hall and across from us. Leigh approached the door and opened it to find another tight stairway that went straight up. "We've come this far," she said, as she forged ahead to lead us the rest of the way.

As we ascended the stairs, the lighter and brighter it became. The top of the stairs opened up into a room… and what a room it was! We must have been on a third floor as we were very high up and could see the tops of trees beneath us through the many bayside windows. The room had a large heavy oak table and chairs in the center that could have easily seated twelve people. Against one wall on the left were wooden crates filled with half-gallon jars with clear sparkling liquid and five-gallon metal cans. There must have been fifty crates stacked up and covered with dust. In the corner, were stacked burlap bags filled with who knows what. An old dark armoire graced the wall on the right, and there was what seemed like another built-in cabinet just behind it.

"Oh wow!" Leigh exclaimed.

Mom went to the windows to look out as Carly and I explored what was on a small pedestal wood table on the inside back wall. A newspaper *The Star* dated *March 18, 1938* was folded and a very small article reporting on the death of E. W. Marler was circled in pencil, the pencil lying beside it. There was also a gold pocket watch and heavy metal large mug.

"Look at this, Leigh!" I couldn't believe it. Of all the newspapers and all the dates, this one had to be on that table… and with that article circled.

Leigh came over. "Our first clue!" she exclaimed as she held the newspaper up and looked over at my mom.

Mom had gone over to the armoire and was trying to push it just a little to expose the built-in cabinet door behind it. "Kristen, Carly, could you help me? I want to move this armoire back and see what's behind that cabinet door."

"Sure, Mom." I felt like we were all fellow sleuths in crime.

When we moved the armoire and Mom opened the cabinet door, we were surprised to see that it had been a hidden doorway onto a widow's walk. From the widow's walk, you could clearly see up and down the bay.

Mom turned back and glanced at the exterior wall of the house only to spot another cabinet door that, when opened, exposed an old lantern and matches.

"Our second clue," Mom said.

At that point, Carly and I knew that we were not going anywhere for a little while, even if the rain stopped, so we went back down, together of course, and fetched all our sandwiches.

On the way back up, Carly spotted a blanket. "Kristen, let's take this for our picnic lunch. That table's so dusty and dirty."

I agreed and grabbed the blanket as her hands were full.

What a day this had been! As we all sat around in a circle, eating our lunch on the blanket, we vowed not to tell anyone about our new discovery. Leigh put her arm in, and then we all followed suit.

"Wait," Carly said, "I have something better than that. "Let's toast," she said, as she pulled a bottle of wine out of her backpack.

Leave it to Carly, I thought. The love that filled me that day as I sat with my friends will stay with me forever.

> *Mom, Leigh, Carly and me,*
> *Best friends we'll always be.*

Well, it finally stopped raining late in the afternoon, and we lazily made our way down the shore and back home, a secret between us.

It was a quarter till eight as I glanced at the clock when we arrived home through the kitchen door. Mom headed straight for the shower.

"Kristen, do you mind if I take my shower first?" Our little frame bungalow just had one bathroom.

"No, Mom. As a matter of fact, I think I still have time to go down to Miss Ada's shop and pick up that picture I had framed for Brett. You go ahead. I'll take mine when I get back."

Brett Hansen was the love of my life. We had known each other since kindergarten, but I hadn't really noticed him until middle school. Everyone knew we were an item and would marry one day. At least, that was the plan. I thought of Brett as I traveled down the road in my little *"Chitty,"* the name I had given my old mid-eighties Dodge Lancer. I thought of how Brett and I had become closer this past year, probably because I was nearing the end of my studies to become an attorney and felt the pressure letting up. Now, we had time to think about us.

As I pulled into the drive behind the store, that let down feeling overcame me as I noticed there were no other cars in the drive. Had I come too late?

I opened Chitty's car door and slid hurriedly out to see if I could catch someone in.

The bells hanging on the wide wooden door jingled as I entered. I made it, I thought. Someone is here. Just then, I see Ada's son, Billy Ray. He was one to stay away from if ever there was one. Billy Ray's dad left when he was just a young boy, and Ada had her hands full with three sons. Billy Ray was the oldest, about eight years older than me and tall and very big. He ended up getting licensed to become an interstate truck driver, and we didn't see him in town much, only when he came back to visit his mother.

"Is Ada here?" I asked when Billy Ray approached from back in the shop.

"No, you just missed her."

"I'll come back," I said. "She was framing a picture for me."

"Let me see," Billy Ray said as he motioned for me to follow him. I must have caught him locking up. I followed him as he closed the front windows and locked the door. Then, we were on our way to the back of the store.

Maybe she had my framed picture ready for me with my name on it in the back, I thought.

I followed him as we entered the back room and then… *slam,* he had me on the cot Ada had made up for when she stayed over or needed to take a nap. Before I knew it, he was on top of me and in me and heavy, very very heavy. It was all so fast… and then it was done. He climbed off of me, hot and sweaty and fastened his clothes. I felt like I had been hit by a truck. I had screamed and screamed, but no one heard me. I grabbed my clothes and got dressed, and he said, "If you ever tell anyone, I will send you home in a box."

That was the beginning of the end of life as I knew it on the Cape. By the time the sun rose the next morning, I had packed a small bag and was on my way to I didn't know where. That was when I left my childhood home on the Cape and moved to Tampa almost three years ago.

Four

It was only my second day back home on the Cape and I awoke with more pain in my back than I could bear. I slipped into the kitchen to find Mom making coffee and mixing up pancake batter. I went directly to the phone at the end of the counter.

"What's the name of that doctor you want me to see? Do you have his number?" I danced around in pain as I held the phone, anxiously waiting for the number. "If I'm going to fight this cancer, I need to get started," I said.

"Dr. Kerns. His number is right there on the little tablet by the phone. I think your appointment is scheduled for tomorrow."

"I can't wait that long, Mom. I can't stand the pain! He has to see me today!"

Mom dusted her hands off on her apron, came across the room, and took the phone from me. "I'll call him," she said.

There was no specialist for small cell cancer patients as the disease was so rare. Dr. Kerns was the lung cancer specialist and CEO of the Cancer Center my cousin Rebecca worked at, and she highly recommended him as small cell cancer was known to originate in the lungs. My cousin was also a cancer doctor at the Center. She knew Dr. Kerns well and paved the way for me to see him. Mom was not able to reach Dr. Kerns right away, so she called Rebecca who was able to reach him and get an appointment for me later that morning.

We felt blessed to have an appointment at any time with this prestigious doctor, but I was impatient because of my pain. I sat down at the kitchen table to eat my pancakes and drink my coffee, but I had to get up and down, dancing around the kitchen, as somehow that would alleviate my pain… naught. Jacob was at the table eating his breakfast, and I could tell he felt for me. My beloved brother Jacob, how I hated hurting him. How I hated that he had to go through this.

My oldest brother Johnny, John Michael Parker, Jr., had married Angela "Angie" Tanner, and they lived in town to be by the docks for his seafood and trucking business. Johnny and I were close as we were just five years apart. I was the older sister, and Johnny my younger brother. We had been comrades as we grew up together. Jacob came along twelve years later after Johnny. When I thought of Johnny now, I was glad that he was not here, at home, at breakfast with us. I don't think he could have handled seeing me in so much pain. Johnny, too, would probably agree.

Mom looked tortured as she watched me. "Kristen, what would help your pain? Would it help to have an ice pack and lie down or be up and active?" She asked this as I had been constantly getting up and dancing around the house. I didn't know what to tell her. I didn't know what would help. I just knew I needed pain relief right away.

"I wish we could have gotten in sooner," Mom said. "Maybe there's a reason, though, why we are supposed to go at the later time this morning. Mom quoted her favorite Bible verse that up until now she had used to get her through hard times – *Romans 8:28*

> *And we know that in all things God works for the good of those who love him, who have been called according to his purpose.*

"Mom, I love the Lord," I said, and then asked with a little sarcasm, "but how could this possibly work together for my good, a young woman who loves the Lord? How could delaying treating my pain even one minute be for my good?"

"I don't know, Kristen, but we don't always see the larger picture. Maybe you're supposed to meet someone there who wouldn't be there earlier this morning. I don't know, but I do believe it. Maybe it will be revealed to us later."

The Cancer Center was about an hour's drive from home, and I was hoping my dad would take us in the family camper. It would be much more comfortable for me as I could get up and down and walk around when I needed to.

"Where is Dad this morning?" I asked.

"Oh, he's down at his workshop building a boat, his latest project."

My eyes rolled as I got up from my chair at the table to take a walk down and see him. There he was, actually sitting across from his partially-built boat and just staring at it, a cup of coffee in his hand. The boat was framed out of cypress and he had pine for the decks.

"Hi, Dad."

"Hi, Kristen."

"Mom got me an appointment at the Cancer Center later this morning, and I was wondering if you'd drive us in the camper. My back's hurting, and I could get up and walk around instead of having to stay seated."

Dad looked over at his boat, put his hand to his chin, raised it, and squinted the left side of his face as if he had to contemplate. "Well, I need to get this boat done," he said, and then added after a pause, "but yes, I could. About what time do we need to go?"

"Well, it's about an hour away, and I'd like to be there early, so how about as soon as we can get ready?"

"OK. Is Miss Queen Bee going with us?" *Queen Bee* is what Dad called little Briana. Once upon a time, I had been his *Princess*, so I guess it only followed that Briana would be *Queen Bee*.

"Yes, Dad, I want Mom to come, so Briana has to come, too."

"I'll get the camper out and be up to the house in a few."

"Great," I said as I walked back thinking how hard could it be to make a decision to take your daughter to her first appointment at the Cancer Center? What project could be more important?

We arrived at the Cancer Center early as I had hoped we would. When we entered the waiting area, patients were watching the television screen as firemen and rescue workers were sifting through the devastation left by 9/11. The estimated count of victims was at least 2,900. I wondered how many victims there were of cancer. How many people had died on 9/11 of cancer? How many had even been told on 9/11, like I had been, that their diagnosis was cancer, terminal cancer?

Dr. Kerns seemed to be a very professional and kind man. He didn't hold any punches though. He basically confirmed what I had already been told... that I had small cell cancer, and it was terminal. He didn't, however, take my hope away. He conveyed to me, and I believed him, that he would fight it with everything he and the Center had to fight it with.

As I was leaving, I stopped and asked him, "Dr. Kerns, how many people do you think die each day from cancer?"

"Kristen, I would estimate more than 500,000 people die each year from cancer."

"Oh my!" I exclaimed. In my wildest imagination, I would never have thought it was that high.

"And how many people do you think are diagnosed each day with cancer?"

"Probably more than a million each year," he said.

I did a mental calculation in my head. A million divided by 365 days a year. That's about the same number of people being diagnosed with cancer each day as the number of victims of 9/11.

What I most liked about Dr. Kerns that day was that he sent me right over to the Infusion Center for emergency steroids to stop my pain, or at least put a dent in it. I was told that I was given forty times the amount of steroids they normally give a patient. Guess I was an emergency.

The Infusion Center was a large room with lots of green plastic-covered high-back recliner chairs. The chairs were arranged in such a way as to encourage social communication with other patients or with the person who came with you. I was assigned a nurse who would carry out the orders of my doctor, which today was injecting me with steroids through an intravenous tube.

"Hi, I'm Cathy, your nurse for today. This," she said as she motioned to a woman sitting next to me and then one across from me, "is Abby and Martha."

I was thankful for the social introductions as Mom had taken Briana over to the cafeteria, and Dad had gone to gas up the camper.

"Hi, I'm Kristen," I announced. I felt like I was joining a club, a club that had so many members, a club I didn't want to join, and this was the initiation. I felt like my life was out of my control, and I had been bumped onto a moving path like the one at the airport or Universal Studios, and on the path were many tasks I had to complete. This was just one of them.

Martha was an older lady, probably about sixty-five, and Abby wasn't much older than I was. They were both receiving something intravenously and acted as though it were no more out of the ordinary than stopping to put gas in your car.

My mind wanted to scream, "I just joined this club, and this isn't normal!" I wanted to fight this cancer.

Martha was the first to speak. She was knitting what looked like a baby blanket. Maybe it was for one of her grandchildren, or an expected grandchild. It was beautiful with greens and yellows. It must be for an expected grandchild, I thought, who she doesn't know if it will be a baby boy or girl.

"Where are you from?" she asked.

"I'm from the Cape, Cape San Blas, near Apalachicola."

"Oh, my husband and I used to live in Eastpoint, just east of Apalachicola, years ago. He made his livin' as an oysterman and fisherman. Some weeks, he'd go out on Sunday and not be back in till Thursday. Then, he'd expect me to start shuckin'. I put up with that for many years and then told him that it was either me or his boat. Fortunately, he had the good sense to choose me. Then, we moved over further east to Wakulla County, have a nice little house in St. Marks."

"I've actually been living in Tampa and working in the city as a paralegal. I came home when I learned I had terminal small cell cancer."

"Oh, dear. How old are you?"

"I'll be thirty soon. Some present, isn't it? And I have a beautiful little girl who is almost two."

That was enough for Abby to speak up. "I know how you feel," she said. "I'm only thirty-three. I don't have any children yet, but I wanted to. Now, I don't know what will happen."

I learned that Abby had Stage IV Non-Hodgkin's lymphoma. She had bone marrow biopsies with giant needles and was receiving chemotherapy daily. She put her hand on her head and unabashedly slipped her short wig off. She was bald, bare bald. She sat directly across from me and smiled as her eyes sparkled. For some reason, we both burst into laughter. I knew Abby and I were going to become good friends.

Maybe, I wondered, I was meant to meet Abby to be her friend, to be here for her, not the other way around. I couldn't wait to tell Mom. Maybe there was a reason why my appointment had been at this time, and maybe it was to be a friend to Abby.

I wasn't at the Infusion Center long as receiving my steroids, even forty times the normal amount, only took about fifteen minutes. I would later get radiation to shrink the tumors and then begin chemotherapy treatments.

Mom came in just before I was ready to be released. "Bri's with Dad in the camper," she said. I introduced her to Martha and Abby, and then we left.

Dr. Kerns had written out many prescriptions for medication that we needed to stop and turn in at a pharmacy. There was medication for pain like oxycodone and oxycontin, one was short-lasting, and one was long-lasting. There were sleeping pills and anti-anxiety medication like lorazepam, and there was anti-nausea medication for when I began chemotherapy again.

As we drove back home, I held Briana tight and thought about Abby. I wondered if she would beat her cancer and live to have a marriage and children one day. I thought about my special Briana. I wanted to do everything with her, but how do you do twenty years of activities in the short number of days I might have left?

"Mom, do you think you and Dad could drop me and Briana off at the park in Apalachicola while ya'll get my prescriptions filled?"

Mom looked at Dad and Dad looked at Mom. "Sure, Kristen, that would be fine."

As Briana and I stepped out of the camper at the park, I faintly heard the melody of the ice cream truck as it neared the playground area. I rushed with Bri in the direction of where it seemed headed. As the colorful step-van traveled down the road, its melody brought all the children who were not at the park from their houses. Some were with their mothers. Some were by themselves with money their mothers had given them to buy ice cream or popsicle treats. Briana was not even old enough to ask for ice cream, but I felt the urgency.

As the ice cream truck pulled up aside the playground, you could sense the excitement in the children. A short line formed as they waited and looked at the colorful pictures of pops on the side of the truck.

"What would you like, Briana?" I held her up as we stood beside the step-van and looked at all the pictures. She pointed to a colorful cherry popsicle. It was all I could do as I hugged her and pulled her closer to me not to cry. I could feel an avalanche waiting to happen.

We sat on a tree stoop and ate our popsicles, Briana her cherry and me a banana. There was cherry flavored juice all over Briana, on her face and hands, and I thought she never looked more beautiful. I wanted to see that face forever.

Then, I took Briana's hand and walked over to the swings. The baby swings were empty, so I slid Briana in one and began to push her through my tears. She didn't seem to like to swing, but wasn't that an experience that mothers and daughters shared? I hadn't spent time in Tampa taking Briana to the park; I had spent time working. I didn't have time now to come to the park on different occasions for her to slowly become used to the swing. There wasn't time. The doctor's, now two doctors', prognosis resounded in my mind, and my heart, and my soul. There wasn't time.

Briana pointed to some children playing on some other playground equipment. She did not seem to want to swing, so I lifted her out of the swing and set her down to run and play with the other children. I sat on a nearby park bench that must have been designed for mothers like me. How I enjoyed watching her play.

"Do people ever die from a broken heart?" I wondered. Perhaps that is what is happening to me. Perhaps my body had all the heartache it could take and manifested cancer. Perhaps this cancer is pain that had to show up some way. Now, it's my reality. The heartache had been my reality, but I stuffed it down. I ran away from the Cape to Tampa. I got busy to help me stuff it. Maybe cancer is caused from a broken heart. The only saving grace has been my precious little girl. I smile as I watch her bouncing from the monkey bars to the see-saw and back again.

As Mom and Dad pulled up in the camper, I wondered if I would ever stop crying? What an emotional day it had been. I pulled myself together to look as if I hadn't been crying, although there were still tears on the inside. I called my beautiful little daughter, took her hand, and we went home with all my many prescriptions.

Five

The days in September seemed to fly by. Not only was there 9/11, that fateful day, in September but also my brother Jacob's thirteenth birthday on September 21st and my little Briana's second birthday on September 24st. Soon after I received the steroids, I began the radiation and chemotherapy regimen. I was so tired, so very very tired, all the time.

Mom usually had a birthday party at the house for Jacob and his best buds. This year, however, she had it at the closest movie theater which was in Panama City. After they saw the movie, Mom had a scavenger hunt list ready for them. They divided into two teams, Jacob the team captain of one and another team captain whom Jacob chose. Then, the captains chose their teams. The list had items that could be gathered from the movie theater shopping center and parking lot. At home, she would have had a clothes pin from a neighbor's yard, a toilet paper roll, and a live chameleon from outside, things like that on the list. Now, she had things like a menu from a restaurant (there was a diner on the corner of the shopping center), a past due bill (needed from some patron's purse), and an old candy wrapper (that could probably be found on the sidewalk). Each team's list had ten items, the same items but in different order which they may or may not discover during the competition. The boys had fun and the winning team received free movie passes to come back again with a friend. Mom had included me in helping her think up items for the list, but I was asleep or passed out in my bed at home during his party. At least, that's what I was told. Leigh came and stayed with me and played with Briana till they all came home.

Briana's party was much simpler. We invited a few friends with children and took her to the park in Apalachicola, complete with picnic lunch, balloons, and birthday cake. We were able to plan it for when I was feeling a little better, a short alert spurt in an afternoon.

Next was my birthday, October 24th. I would be thirty, the big 3-0. It was over a year since my initial diagnosis of cancer, the supposedly breast cancer I thought I had survived. A lot had happened since then.

Usually, Mom and I try to outdo each other when it's our birthday. We're best friends after all and we've tried to do everything we can to promote one another's dreams. The year Mom turned forty back in 1990, I gave her money in her birthday card and wrote that it was to be used toward an Outward Bound sailing course that set sail from Key West. Mom had been lookin' at that Outward Bound catalog for about ten years, and they had a course that was just for women over thirty. Jacob had just been born a little over a year earlier, but I would watch Mom look at that catalog year after year, and I thought she should go. Mom's birthday gifts to me were just as special, gifts extraordinaire. Last year, after I had endured my first cancer diagnosis and treatment in Tampa, Mom gave me the gift to top all gifts.

It was the alternate year of the FSU – Gator game that would be played at the Seminole Campbell Stadium in Tallahassee. The Florida State University Seminoles in Tallahassee and the University of Florida Gators from Gainesville were rivals… big time rivals. I remembered all the games I used to go to with my family when I grew up on the Cape and then with my friends when I began school in Tallahassee, especially the annual FSU – Gator game. I wanted to make arrangements to go to this game. I had just had my cancer *scare* and was fighting the winning battle, or so I thought, but I had this uneasiness, a sense that it may be my last chance to attend this game.

I bought airline tickets to Tallahassee so I wouldn't have to miss much work, made arrangements for a friend from work to take care of Bri, and proceeded to buy tickets for the game. Everywhere I tried, I came up with a dead end. I should have known that the famed FSU-Gator game would be sold out. I tried everywhere. I even checked for scalp 'em priced tickets. There just were none to be had. I was so disappointed.

When I talked with Mom on the phone and expressed my disappointment, she suggested that I plan for next year's FSU – Gator game.

"It just wouldn't be the same," I proclaimed. "Next year, it will be in Gainesville. It's just not the same as Doak Campbell Stadium when the Indian rides out on Renegade in garnet and gold colors and we all release our balloons into the air. It's just not the same."

"Well," my mother said, "you could plan ahead and go in two years when the game is back at Campbell Stadium in Tallahassee."

I'm not sure why I said this, but the words just came tumbling out… "Mom, I don't even know if I'll be here."

That was kind of that, and we didn't talk about it again. I assumed it was because my mother knew how depressed I was about it.

Then, it was my birthday, my 29th birthday. I opened a card from my mother only to find another, although very professional looking, card inside. It was a rich cream color with a thin garnet strip on the left-hand side of the envelope. Printed within the vertical garnet strip were gold letters spelling out *Florida State University*. In the left-hand corner of the envelope, it read –

Office of the President
Florida State University
Tallahassee, FL 32306-1350

This was from the Office of the President at Florida State University? My name appeared in the center of the envelope – *Kristen Parker*. I paused as I pondered what I had just seen, my curiosity peaking.

I opened the envelope and took out a garnet and gold card with the Seminole Tribe of Florida's emblem on the front that signified Sacred Fire and their unconquered spirit. When I opened the card, it was even more incredible. On the entire left-hand side was a picture of Seminole Chief Osceola riding Renegade, his left arm raised holding the burning spear that is planted at the beginning of every game on the fifty-yard line. Renegade was rearing up with him in front of the Florida State University seal. I glanced to the right at a printed invitation –

In recognition of your
Outstanding Devotion and Support of
Florida State University
President Talbot D'Alemberte
offers
Kristen Parker
Two Football Tickets
when

Florida State University
plays
University of Florida

Saturday, November 18, 2000

It was unbelievable! I then opened a folded piece of notebook paper on which my mother had written her note –

Dear Kristen,
    I wanted you to be surprised. On a Friday, eleven days before your birthday, the president's office

at F.S.U. responded to my letter. They said I could purchase tickets they were reserving for legislators. You know they must be good seats. Anyway, I'm glad we were able to make this happen for you, and I know God had something to do with it. Always remember I love you, and anything is possible with God.

Have a very happy birthday!

Love,

Mom

Needless to say, what could have been better! By the way, FSU won that game. As Mom said, "All things are possible with God."

And now, as I sit on the front steps of my childhood home, I wonder what could top that? Mom, do you have a magic wand you can pull out of a hat? Can you give me life... again? Can you give me *time*? I don't think so.

And, yes, I believe that all things are possible with God. I believe that he can heal me, but will he? I don't know.

I can smell the fresh sea air. It is so inviting. I want to cross over the dunes and walk along the shore, but I am so very, very tired.

* * * * *

It was about nine-thirty that evening when Johnny walked in. We were all sitting around the living room. I was lying on the sofa.

"Hi, *Son*, what are you doing here this late?"

"Just thinkin' about you and wanted to talk. Let's go upstairs."

Johnny's bedroom had been the upstairs attic room, a sprawling room with high pitched roof and exposed rafters. When we were young, we had spent countless hours debating our life predicaments outside his window on the tin roof looking at the stars.

"There's a full moon out tonight," Johnny said as he went for the window in the front of his old bedroom to open it. "Let's talk outside."

As I climbed out the bedroom window, following Johnny, and onto the tin roof, I felt as though I was a teenager again and Johnny's very competent older sister. Now, however, I was disabled. I had cancer, terminal cancer at that.

Johnny had been right. It was a full moon, and one of the largest moons I had ever seen. It shone so brightly that we could almost see across the peninsula to the beach… and if we were quiet, we could faintly hear the sound of the waves gently crashing against the shore.

We sat quietly for a moment, both of us with our knees up under our chin, our arms wrapped around our knees, leaning up against the old bedroom window and front of the house. Then, Johnny said in his sweet way that bordered on humor, that only the two of us could understand, "It's a bum rap, Kristen." Then, he added, "How could God let this happen?"

I thought before I answered.

"*Son*, I don't think God's responsible for this. *Cause and effect, Son*," I said adding a little humorous tone myself that only he would understand. "Kind of like if you have a drunken driver that runs a red light and kills some innocent person. Cause and effect, I don't think God is responsible for everything."

"But Kristen, you don't deserve it," he said emphatically.

"*Now Son*, it's naïve of me to think things should go smooth my whole life, which by the way is an understatement of how my life has been the last three years. When something unexpected happens, most people ask why. The question should be – why not? *Son*, when we are born, we do not have a note attached to us proclaiming that only our short-sighted plans are allowed to happen the rest of our lives. We, after all, cannot claim fame for the fact that we were even born. And *Son*, how many other people live on this planet doing heaven only knows what? Why do we always act like we have control? Or even should have? Life is not always the way we wish it were. It's the way it is. The only control we have is how we handle it, and that makes all the difference."

"But Kristen, it's so unfair."

"I know, but Mom always says from Romans 8:28 – All things work together for good for those who love the Lord. Oh no, I sound like Mom now. Anyway *Son*, there must be a reason."

We sat there looking at the clear dark sky and listening to the distant sea waves. Was there any time more precious than this moment with my brother?

Six

One of our old haunts was the pizzeria in Apalachicola on Market Street. Carly and I had been spending time there since we had been young adolescents in middle school casing out the boys. We had also met there to discuss whatever dilemma we happened to be involved in at the time, so it was no wonder when she called and asked me if I could meet her that we quite naturally thought of our old hangout. When I arrived, I went straight to our booth as I had seen her through the window. The menu was already on the table before me, but I glanced at Carly and confirmed that I'd go for our usual, a cheese pizza with extra oregano.

When I looked up, my eyes caught a glimpse of Brett. He was leaning over at the end of the counter talking to Mary Jo, his left leg crossed over his right, *and in those tight fitting faded blue jeans* – does nothing ever change! His chest was bare and tanned and toned, and his fishin' theme T-shirt was slung over his shoulder. Brett's eyes are the blue of the sky on a clear day, so intense yet they can dance at a moment's notice. And his hair… his sandy blonde bangs were always just a little too long and pushed over to one side, causing him to give that little flip of his head every now and then to toss them back.

Mary Jo was waiting on a customer, ringing up the bill on that old cash register that came over on the Mayflower. Brett was just casually leaning on the counter and providing what seemed like small talk.

When I left the Cape, Brett had been working with his father in his construction business. His father had slowly been giving him more of the responsibility and leadership of the crew. Maybe Brett was on his lunch break from a nearby construction job.

"Carly," I asked as I motioned over to Brett with a discreet nod of my head, "what's Brett's story these days? Is he still working construction for his father?"

"No, Old Man Farley finally retired, and Brett became the new building inspector. I think he sometimes still helps his father though when he can."

"What about a woman in his life?"

"I know Brett's dated occasionally, but no one serious. Kristen, he hasn't been serious about anyone since you left."

I flashbacked to the note I had left him almost three years ago.

> *My dearest Brett,*
> *I need to go away for a while. It's something I must do. Please do not ask why. Please do not try to find me.*
> *Kris*

Just then, our waitress came over. I recognized her as someone who I had gone to high school with, but who was maybe in a lower grade, maybe a year or two or even three younger.

"May I take your order?"

"Yes, we'll have one cheese pizza with extra oregano," Carly said, "and two glasses of white wine." Leave it to Carly to order wine.

"Anything else? Any appetizers?"

"No, that'll do it," I said.

Carly slid across the booth and rose from her seat. "I'm going to the ladies' room," she called over her shoulder as she headed to the back of the restaurant.

The pizzeria was full, so I didn't think Brett would notice me. I sat back and pondered him and the way I felt about him. Maybe it wasn't just Brett whom I loved but the way I had been able to love him… with abandon. It was so intoxicating. Brett wasn't just his youthful gorgeous self. I was contained within him, and I yearned for that earlier time when life was so simple. I wanted to know what we had again, how it felt to be me when I loved him. I wanted to feel his firm arms around me again. As I glanced back over at him, I couldn't help but think… what a gorgeous hunk of man!

Then it happened, our eyes locked. The price I'd pay for glancing back. He looked startled and after a moment started walking over.

"Kristen," he said softly after he had slid into Carly's seat. "Kristen, I have missed you."

I looked at him and didn't know what to say, where to begin.

"Are you here alone?"

"No, I'm with Carly."

"Carly, I should have known."

"Kristen, can I see you? Can we talk?"

"Yes, but I don't know when. I'm staying at home with Mom and Dad and my brother Jacob."

"Can I call you?"

"Yes." And then he was gone. He slid out of Carly's seat and out the door as quietly as he had slid in. And I hoped… I hoped he would call me.

When Carly came back, she was ready for answers. She knew I had kept in touch with Mom by phone after I left the Cape, but why, why hadn't I kept in touch with her? The truth of the matter was that I was still shell shocked. My life had been taken out of my control. I didn't know what to say or do about what had happened that night so long ago. As we sat in our booth at the pizzeria, I told Carly everything.

"Kristen, we have been friends since forever. Didn't you know that I would be here no matter what? Didn't you know that I would help you figure things out?"

No, I didn't at the time, but it was all so clear to me now.

"Carly, please forgive me."

The waitress came over with our glasses of wine. "Your pizza will be out in just a minute," she said. "Can I get you anything else while you're waiting?"

"No, I think we have everything we need now," Carly said as she smiled and looked at me. "Kristen, I am so glad you're back."

The waitress seemed to understand that this was a reunion of friends. "Be right back with your pizza," she said as she jaunted off to the kitchen.

When she had left, our conversation turned serious.

"Kristen, have you ever thought about pressing charges against Billy Ray?"

"Not at first, but countless times over the past few years. I wonder if he has ever done that before to anyone else. I wonder if I had pressed charges if maybe I could have saved another woman from having it happen to her. The only thing is, I don't want him to even know about Briana."

"We'll come up with something," Carly said, and you could tell she had her thinking cap on. "Don't worry, Kris, we'll come up with something."

Just then, the pizza arrived. It looked as good as I had remembered it being. Biting into the first slice confirmed it. Aah, the simple pleasures in life – friends and pizza.

As we left the pizzeria, we compared notes on where we had parked our cars. They were both parked around the corner from Market Street on Avenue D. It was the beginning of October and the weather was perfect, not too hot like our North Florida summers but not yet too cold. As we turned the corner and began to walk to our cars, my eyes darted over to a couple coming out of the River Oasis. It was Dad and Miss Viola Peters! At first, I stood there in shock, and then whispered to Carly, "Let's follow them."

The River Oasis is a bar where the local fishermen hang out. It can be rough and not a place that I would choose to go to with my friends. And Viola Peters… even her name, *Peters*, how much more appropriate could that be?

As she and my dad walked down the street with her arm in his, she was hanging all over him, wearing a tight-fitting leopard print mini-skirt with low cleavage and high heeled shoes. Her beehive hairdo gave her age away. They were so engrossed in conversation that they didn't notice us as we followed them, obviously on their way to a certain destination. Finally, they reached Water Street and crossed the road to the Riverfront Inn. I couldn't believe my eyes.

Seven

When I look back on my life, I suppose I always knew I wanted to study law and work for the underdog and fight for justice, justice for all, not just for the prominent and wealthy. I remember as a small girl of about seven growing up on the Cape learning for the first time that the world was not always a safe place, that not everyone had my best interest, or the best interest of others, at heart.

That was the year of my first encounter with an endangered species needing my help to protect it long enough to have a chance at life. "Matilda" made such an impression on me that summer and commanded all my attention and effort. Matilda, you see, was a loggerhead sea turtle. I watched her as she came ashore to lay her eggs. Such determination I had never seen. It took her days to find the perfect place, but little did she know about the Johnson brothers.

They would destroy anything in their path. The Johnson brothers didn't always live on the Cape. Their father, Brody Johnson, had been moving his family up to Thomasville, Georgia, earlier that year when their truck broke down on the State Road 30 stretch between Apalachicola and Port St. Joe. He needed work to pay for the repairs, and Old Man Hawkins gave him a job working on his shrimp boat. Widow Jenkins on the Cape had plenty of space and let the family bunk in the room above her bayside boat house.

It has been said that sea turtles return every two to four years to their native beach that proved successful in nesting and launching their offspring. Little did Matilda know that the terrain on her beach had changed – it now included the Johnson brothers.

This was back in the day when I was Dad's "princess." He had set up four markers around Matilda's nesting site when he was home from oysterin' so that I could watch for the little hatchlings to emerge from the egg chamber and make their journey down to the shore. Every morning during the summer, I would make my way down the path to the beach and survey the nesting site to see if anything had changed. Every night at dusk, I would beg Ma to take me down and see if the hatchlings were stirring, ready to break through the sand and begin their journey by moonlight to the water. It was mid August, and Matilda had laid her eggs in early June. This massive sea turtle had gone back into the sea, and I had vowed to watch her nesting site. It was as if I was the expectant mother.

"Stop! Stop!" I yelled as I ran down the beach one morning toward Matilda's nest, waving and flailing my arms.

In the distance, I could see Jason and Trevor Johnson doing who knows what to the nesting site. Trevor, his name should have been Terror. I could see him stomping his feet around in the sand. Just the week before, I had seen the brothers in action at our church fellowship hall for the after-church social. It looked like a tornado had gone through when they left.

My heart pounded as I raced as fast as I could down the beach to where the boys were. When I reached the nest, the boys had run off. I could see scuffling around the marked site, but nothing looked disturbed inside the markers. I vowed that I would not let anything happen to the nest. Hundreds of little sea turtles were too close to hatching and making their way to the life God had for them. Matilda was counting on me.

That night, I pleaded with Ma not to go in. It was probably the latest night I ever stayed up in my childhood. My younger brother Johnny, two at the time, and I played on the beach. When it became late, he slept on the blanket beside my mother and me as we talked. I think Ma was waiting for me to get sleepy, but then it happened… the first of many little hatchlings poked their heads out of the sand, struggled to the surface, and made a mass exodus to the sea. I was awestruck watching what seemed like hundreds of little sea turtles instinctively making their way toward the reflection of the moon and starlight on the water. They had been protected and hatched in spite of the Johnson brothers.

Years passed, and I would again see a need for protection of rights. This time, it would be the Apalachicola fisherman's rights to make a living and protect their environment. I was a teenager when it happened, and I watched government legislation – a net ban – threaten the livelihood of my family and other families we knew. The oystermen and fishermen and shrimpers we knew all cared about the bay. Most of them had been born and raised on the water, their fathers and grandfathers before them making a living from the sea. They knew more from life and experience than any fact in a book on a government book shelf. I remember nights laying in bed overhearing my dad talk with his fishermen friends about how the ban threatened the very bay they loved. They needed an attorney to protect their way of life and the waters that supported it. They needed an attorney who descended from their culture. I wanted to be that attorney and always knew that someday I would study law.

Eight

I don't know what made me sicker – the cancer or the treatment. Although I was fighting the cancer as hard as I could and believed in my doctor at the Cancer Center, I gave way to the thought that maybe I would die, maybe, as hard as I tried, I would not be able to beat it. I refused to give up, but on this day, October 10, 2001, I began to write a journal for my precious Briana –

> *I don't know a gentler way to say this. My words will never be put together well enough for you to read. I need to tell you this, though…*

I wondered…how do I tell my daughter that when we first arrived at the Cancer Center last month, Dr. Kerns saw that the cancer had spread to different places in my lungs and on my spine in my lower back where I had been having the pain? I wondered how to tell her how serious his words were. Aside from the terminal prognosis, Dr. Kerns told me that I could already have been paralyzed and/or lost control of my bowel and bladder because of the location of the tumor pushing on my spine. That first day, he had given me emergency steroids, Decadron, and then I had twelve complete sessions of radiation. I was now going through my first session of heavy-duty chemotherapy.

I wanted to tell her that I was fighting so very very hard because she was so special to me. I wanted so much to be there for her forever and see her grow up. I wanted to go through each and every cycle of her life and face the different challenges as she got older. As I found words to put on the paper, the underlining I used to give emphasis to certain words did not even begin to measure the intensity of my feelings. The thing that hurt me most was the thought of not being there should my little girl get sick. I tried not to let my tears fall on the journal page as I wrote. I hoped that my writing sounded OK. Sometimes my mind was clear, but sometimes it was foggy from the chemo. I think they call it *chemo brain*.

* * * * *

Dad drove me to most of my chemotherapy treatments. He didn't know that I had seen him with Viola Peters. I knew I needed to talk to Mom, but I didn't know when. It was hard to find a time when we were alone, or I wasn't sleeping.

I arrived at my third chemotherapy treatment, and it seemed like business as usual. I was glad to see that Abby and Martha were there. Thank the Lord for Martha's husband Ollie. He and Dad would usually go over to the cafeteria and get coffee and "shoot the breeze."

"So, what are we having today?" I ask as I slide into a recliner near the girls. "Paclitaxel and Carboplatin or Etoposide?"

Martha smiles and Abby responds with "I'm having Cytoxan, Adriamycin, Vincristine, and Prednisone. I got you beat."

"Oh yum," I said.

I'm not sure how this game got started, but we tried to outdo each other and see who had the chemotherapy drug with the most excruciatingly long name.

I wondered if Abby and Martha noticed that I was talking as though I had marbles in my mouth. Although this was only my third chemo treatment, my mouth was hurting from little ulcers on my tongue. I had been equipped at home with a mouthwash to swish and swallow that was supposed to numb my mouth. It wouldn't take the symptom of the chemo away, just camouflage it.

"So, how's Bri?" Abby asked.

"Oh, she has been so sweet. She knows when Mommy's back is hurting, and she comes over and whispers, 'Mommy's back's hurting,' as she tenderly pats me."

"It must be wonderful having a little girl. Is your mother watching her at home today?"

"No, Mom had to go to work, so I've got her in a little preschool on weekdays. That's why Dad has been bringing me to chemo most of the time."

Just then, a woman I had never seen made her way across the room to us. She looked healthy and professional, carrying an 8½ by 11 tablet in a leather portfolio at her side, so I assumed she worked at the Center.

As she got closer, she made eye contact with all three of us.

"Hi, I'm Janet Miller, a social worker here. I just wanted to stop by and introduce myself and see if there is any way I can help you."

Abby and Martha and I all looked at one another.

"Not unless you're giving away cures today," Abby said with a gleeful smile. Even with all she had been going through, Abby was a bright spot in my day when I came in for treatment.

I told the social worker that I began journaling for my little daughter, "but," I said as I raised my hand and pointed my index finger high, "I am fighting this cancer and I plan on winning. Hopefully, we can read my journal together one day."

"Well, anything I can help you with," she said as she was about to leave, "anything at all."

Without thinking, I stopped her. "Yes, there may be something. Do you know how I would report a rape? Do you know of any attorney, or do I need to go to the county prosecutor?"

She looked at me questioningly.

I told her that it had not been recent, but, yes, I had been raped. I felt comfortable talking with Abby there, but Martha looked very uncomfortable. She looked like she wanted to disappear and just beam out of her chair.

I couldn't believe it myself, that I had said anything. I had been living with fear for the past few years, fear of what had happened and how it changed my life, fear that Billy Ray (and I even hated thinking his name) would come after me and make his threat good, even fear of talking about it. I think I had just decided that it was time to face what happened and put an end to my fear. I also had guilt. What if he had done this to other young women or even a young girl after he had assaulted and raped me, and, even more important, what if there were others who would be raped in the future if he wasn't stopped? I think it was something I wanted to resolve before, heaven forbid, my death.

The social worker gently put her hand on my leg and looked kindly into my eyes. "I think the first step would be to go see the county prosecutor, and maybe you could come to my office one day after your treatment and we could talk."

I don't think she understood that I didn't have time to talk, but I did need to resolve this. I thanked her for the information, and she said she'd see us again.

Dad and Ollie came back from their hiatus, and Martha and her husband left. I knew she was genuinely concerned for me, but people in her day didn't openly talk about rape. I hadn't openly talked about it either until today. Dad escaped again to gas up the camper.

Abby empathized with me. She even knew who Billy Ray was, as she had dated one of his younger brothers at one time. It felt good to finally be able to talk with someone about it. Abby and I were becoming close, and I could feel seeds of love beginning to sprout in my heart for her. She wanted to one day get married and have children, and she didn't yet know what the outcome would be of her lymphoma. She didn't know if she would live long enough to have that chance.

"Abby, do you think you'd like to go to the park with Briana and me sometime, sometime when we're both feeling better?"

"I'd love to," she said, and she smiled that wide smile of hers with eyes sparkling.

As Dad and I were driving home, he told me about Ollie and his experience on the Cape during World War II. An English tanker had been torpedoed by a German U-boat off the coast of Cape San Blas in the early morning hours of June 29, 1942. Ollie and his brother, along with other fishermen, took to their boats and went out to rescue survivors who had abandoned the tanker, the Empire Mica. Some of the survivors were only half dressed as they had been asleep in their bunks.

I thought how strange it was that we were talking about this, and the Twin Towers and Pentagon had just been attacked last month, fifty-nine years later, by terrorists. Dad was a veteran of the Viet Nam War and liked a good war story, but I thought how strange it was that I may not have much time left on this earth, and this is what my dad talks about when we are together. No mention was made by me or Dad of Viola Peters and what I had seen.

As soon as we arrived home, and Dad pulled the camper up in the drive, I promptly got out and catapulted myself past the edge of the oyster shell drive, fell to the grass, and was the sickest I had ever been after a treatment. What a sight I must have been, on all fours with my bald head and heaving violently. A Bible verse came to my mind – *Not only so, but we also rejoice in our sufferings, because we know that suffering produces perseverance; perseverance, character; and character, hope.* I wondered if this is what the Bible meant by suffering – all the pain, doctors' appointments, brutal chemotherapy treatments, and this scene. I thought of what I must look like and made a determination that this indeed depicted suffering. *Perseverance* – did I have a choice? I just wanted to skip to the *hope* part.

Nine

It wasn't long before Brett called and wanted to stop by. I was thankful that it was on a day when Mom was at work, Dad was off doing who knew what, Jacob was at school, and little Briana was at her new preschool. I had time to shower, put on the new wig that had been donated through the American Cancer Society and drink a Mountain Dew and Dr. Pepper to help me wake up and look as with it and normal as I could.

Brett appeared at the front door, looking his gorgeous self. He was wearing clean faded blue jeans and a light blue oxford shirt that brought out the color of his eyes, his shirttail hung out over his jeans, with hands in his pockets. You could see the definitive lines of his toned body under his shirt. The first thing Brett did when I opened the screen door and ushered him in was put his arms around me, and we just stood there quietly in a soft embrace for what seemed like not long enough. When we finally released, and he stepped back, he displayed that smile that only belonged to him.

"Brett, it is so good to see you," I said as we made our way to sit down on the sofa. I turned to him and said, "I have missed you so much!"

"Kristen, talk to me. Why did you leave? I talked with your mother, and she told me you were OK, but that was about all I could get out of her. She is so loyal to you. I didn't know where you were. I looked at all the old places we used to go. I even went to Tallahassee on the days you had classes. I didn't know where else to look."

I decided it was time to come clean with what happened. Did I have any choice? No, I didn't, not that I could see.

"Brett, I was raped." Even the word *raped* was hard for me to say, but there it was, out in the open.

He looked at me, his fist in his hand.

A deep sigh came involuntarily from me, and I continued to explain. "The night I left, I had gone to Miss Ada's shop to pick up a picture I was having framed for you. Remember that picture Carly took of us on the main gallery of the old lighthouse?"

Brett nodded.

"Well, I had it blown up and matted in an old paned window frame I got out of Dad's workshop. Anyway, it was about eight or eight-thirty, and I thought I might catch her there. When I pulled in to the parking around back, there were no cars… but I still thought that maybe I'd catch her. When I went around and into the front door, which was still unlocked, Billy Ray came up to the front from the back. Brett, before I knew what was happening, we were in the back room and… he raped me," I said with a lowered voice.

Brett's jaw clenched, and his right fist thrust into his left hand with such force that I thought he must have broken it.

"Brett, I'm sorry," I said softly.

For a minute, Brett didn't say anything. He just looked down. Then, he lifted his head, turned to me, and said, "Kristen, it's not your fault. You didn't do anything wrong."

"Brett, there's more."

He looked at me and quietly waited. My eyes met his, and I could tell that he was wondering what more there could possibly be.

"I came back, Brett, but not alone. I have a little girl, a beautiful little girl. Her name is Briana, and she just turned two years old."

Brett looked like he didn't know what to say. I took his hand and rose from the sofa to walk him to the 9" X 12" photograph of Briana I had taken at J. C. Penney and was mounted on the dining room wall.

"She *is* beautiful, Kristen. She looks just like you."

"Actually, it's amazing how much she does look like me. I can look at old photographs of me with my long blonde hair, and it's as if it was Briana."

Brett smiled but looked puzzled. "Is there someone in your life, a boyfriend or husband?"

"No, Brett, there hasn't been anyone, but there is more." Did I dare lay the rest on him?

I started walking to our large eat-in kitchen. "Would you like some lemonade? I just made it fresh this morning before you came."

"Sure."

I poured us both tall glasses of lemonade and then said, "Let's go out to the porch."

As we made our way through the house and out the screened door to the front porch, I wondered how on earth I was going to tell him about my cancer and prognosis. We made our way to the left end of the porch and sat on the bench glider, my right foot touching the wooden floorboards to start us moving back and forth.

"There's no easy way to tell you this, Brett." I paused and wasn't sure how to proceed.

"I have cancer, and the doctors, more than one, have told me that it's terminal."

His eyes looked directly into mine, and he said, "I don't understand. What are you saying, Kris?" His face seemed stricken with sadness and pain and shock. I wondered how much more he could take.

"I don't understand it anymore than you do." I wanted to tell him all of it, how I was originally misdiagnosed with breast cancer, had a lumpectomy, then radiation and chemotherapy in Tampa, and then

thought I was cured, a survivor. Somehow, though, I just couldn't bring up breast cancer to the man who was the love of my life, not yet. So, instead, I continued, "It's as if my life is out of my control, but, Brett, have our lives ever been in our control?"

Brett gave me a half smile and wince. "You got that right," he said as he shook his head.

We sat together going back and forth and back and forth for a long time before Brett broke in to the silence.

"Kristen, I'll be here for you. I'm not going anywhere."

"Brett, are you sure, after all this?"

"Let's see, you walk out of my life unexpectedly and have been gone for almost three years. How hard can it be, Kris?" he asked somewhat sarcastically. "I love you."

Just then, we heard the squeaky brakes of the school bus in the distance, and Jacob walked up the drive home from school. He walked up the front porch steps and seemed glad to see Brett over at the house again.

"Hey, man," he said as he walked up and high fived Brett. "Good to see you again." I knew Jacob and Brett had probably seen each other around town a lot since I had been gone, and what he really meant was that it was good to see him back over at the house with me.

A very contented feeling came over me.

Brett glanced at his watch. "Do we need to pick up your daughter from preschool?" he asked.

"No, I've been having hard days from the chemotherapy treatments I've been getting, so Mom either picks her up on her way home from work or Dad sometimes does. They should be getting home any time now."

I was getting tired out. This was the longest I had been up and acting like a normal person in a long time. The chemo treatments kept me feeling drained.

"You didn't have work today?" I asked Brett.

"Yes, but there are some things just more important."

Mom came home with lots of grocery bags in her arms, and Brett helped her carry them into the kitchen. "Brett, how good it is to see you. We are having a small birthday party for Kristen tomorrow evening after dinner. Why don't you come?"

"I'll be here, Mrs. Parker. What time?"

"Why don't we say about seven? On second thought, why don't you come for dinner?"

* * * * *

The day of my birthday finally came, October 24, 2001 – I made it! I was thirty years old, the big 3-0. Mom made my favorite for dinner – homemade macaroni and cheese in a very large deep casserole dish. I had gotten so accustomed to making Kraft macaroni and cheese for Bri and me at my condo in Tampa, I had forgotten how good Mom's homemade recipe was. We had sausage, yum, and hotdogs, one of Bri's favorites, with it.

Jacob and I were setting the dining room table for ten, Mom, Dad, Johnny, his wife Angie, Jacob, Brett, Briana, Leigh, Carly, and me, when Brett arrived. Leigh had come earlier to help Mom with dinner.

Briana went running to the door to see who it was, and I followed her. She looked very inquisitively through the screen door at Brett as he stood there, gift in hand.

As I slowly opened the door, I looked down at Briana and raised my arm out to Brett. "Bri, this is Brett, one of Mommy's very good friends."

Briana smiled and watched as Brett entered and took her little hand as if she was royalty. "Nice to meet you," Brett said as he went down on one knee to meet her gaze.

"Dinner is almost ready," I said as I made my way back to help Jacob set the table.

"What can I do to help?" Brett asked and then didn't wait for an answer. He looked down at Bri and said, "What do you say we help your mommy and Uncle Jacob put the silverware around?"

Bri looked delighted and bounced over to the dining room table.

Brett made his way over to the end of the table and very tenderly gave Bri a few pieces of silverware from the stack there. She wasted no time in going about the task of "helping" Brett put a knife, fork, and spoon at each place setting.

Johnny and Angie arrived soon after, and then Carly.

"Does someone want to go down and get your dad?" my mom asked as she looked at me. "He's down at his workshop working on that boat he's building."

I didn't respond as I was already feeling fatigued and wanted to save my strength for the party, my birthday party that in itself was a miracle this year. Brett looked over and directed his eyes at me as he answered my mother. "I'll go," he said.

Bri went running to my dad as he and Brett entered through the back kitchen door. "Pop Pop, we're having a party."

"I see, I see, Miss Queen Bee," he said as he washed his hands in the kitchen sink. "How's the birthday girl?" he asked as he looked over at me.

"Ready for a party, I'd say."

We all sat down, and Dad offered the blessing. This year, I knew it had more to do with me than anything else. No matter how poor my family may have been over the years, food was never scarce. Dad could always go fishin' and trade fish, grouper, snapper, trout, in Apalach for other staples.

You would have thought it was Thanksgiving, or we were the Walton's at least, with all of us around the table. The food was scrumptious and the talk light and full of laughter. Briana seemed to get along well with Brett, and he looked at her with a somewhat quizzical amazement.

When we were finished with dinner, the phone rang. Mom got up from the table to answer it in the kitchen and then called out to me, "Kristen, it's for you?"

Who could that be? I wondered.

"Kristen speaking," I said when I reached the phone on the kitchen counter.

"Hi, Kristen, it's Terry. I just wanted to call and wish you a happy birthday and let you know that I will be up your way on Saturday over Thanksgiving weekend. I'm going to be staying at the Coombs House Inn in Apalachicola."

I was very surprised to hear from Terry, the corporate attorney I had worked for in Tampa. It was nice to know I was remembered.

"Terry, it's so good to hear from you. When will you arrive?"

"Probably late Friday night. I'm going to take off early and leave straight from work? Would you be up to having breakfast with me at the Inn on Saturday morning, or should I come to your house?"

"Oh Terry, I have good days and bad. Why don't I either meet you for breakfast or call you that morning if it's better for you to come here?"

"Sounds like a plan. Should we say about nine o'clock?"

"That should be fine. Thanks for calling, and I'll either see you at the Inn for breakfast on Saturday or call you before nine."

"I'm looking forward to it. Bye."

"Bye, Terry. See you then."

When I returned to the dining room table, Mom and Leigh started clearing plates. "Let's have the cake in the living room," Mom said. I was getting sweaty from my wig, my face flushed, and I looked at Brett and asked if he'd mind if I took my wig off. Everyone else was used to seeing me with it off, but I had never been in front of Brett yet with my bald head. I think I decided that he either loved me or he didn't, and my bald head was part of me now, at least today.

Brett responded, "I love you with your beautiful natural hair or your bald head. Let's shed the wig."

"I think we need some music," Jacob proclaimed as he made his way across the room. We all followed him.

The large square coffee table was filled with gifts, and Mom brought out a large cake and candles, thirty of them, thirty candles. I think the candles excited me more than anything. The gifts were nice, but what could I do with them if I should die tomorrow? Somehow, they didn't seem as important.

The song *We are Family* by Sister Sledge started to play, and Jacob went over and turned it up. It kind of snapped me out of my daze as I had been looking at the cake and gifts and pondering life. I jumped up and started to dance. That's all the others needed. Little Bri bounced over and started to dance with me, giggling, and Mom joined in. Leigh and Carly both came over and started to dance. Johnny danced with Angie. Brett came over and joined Briana and me, and, Jacob, he danced with Lucky. Lucky got so excited seeing everyone dance that he got up, twirled around and barked. I think it was the most active I have ever seen him. The chorus rang out –

We are family.
I got all my sisters with me.
We are family.
Get up ev'rybody and sing.

Then, the song *Celebrate* by Kool and the Gang came on –

Celebrate good times, come on!
Let's celebrate.
Celebrate good times, come on!
Let's celebrate.

When it got to the verse, I spun around and picked up a large round hairbrush that just happened to be lying on an end table and held it in my hand like a microphone. As the verse started, I sang out…

There's a party goin' on right here,
a celebration to last throughout the years.

It was my time to shine. No one else knew the words to the verse except me. Well, Jacob probably did, and I was sure Brett did, but they let me have the limelight. The song continued as I danced around as a star, the others taking backstage…

So bring your good times and your laughter, too.
We're gonna celebrate a party with you.

Then, we all joined in the chorus. I don't know where my energy came from, but as I looked around at all of us, I realized I was truly happy. It was my birthday, and everyone I loved was here. Mom had topped last year's present… and so had God. I was grateful to God for the very breath I breathed and for all the love that surrounded me.

Ten

The Saturday morning after my birthday, I awoke to the aroma of freshly baked apple pies cooling on the back kitchen window ledge. Faint giggles could be heard from Briana playing with Lucky. "Want some breakfast, Lucky Dog?" she shrieked joyfully. Umm, I thought, slipping up in bed to a sitting position and stretching to greet the morning sun that was shining in through the window. As I reached for my robe and made my way to the kitchen, I could hear the sound of eggs being beaten with a fork in a bowl and the sizzle of bacon.

"Brett called earlier," Mom said as I peeked over her shoulder at all the food that had been prepared before I even stirred. "He said he'd be stopping by later."

I sat down in a chair at the kitchen table in the center of the room and looked over at Briana. "Good morning, Bri," I said. She got up and toddled over, her arms outstretched for a big hug. Once we exchanged a morning hug, she smiled up at me and then made her way back over to Lucky. She picked up Jacob's cap and continued playing dress up with the dog. Lucky was lying on the kitchen linoleum floor, sleeping with his head resting on his front paws. As Briana put Jacob's cap on his head, he raised one eyebrow and then the other without moving an inch.

"Remember, Mom," I said as I looked over at her still busying herself at the stove, "back in the day when Brett would come over on Saturdays and pick me up for a lazy day of fishin'? It was like clockwork."

"Yes, I remember," she answered without looking away from her bacon and eggs. "I didn't dare make any plans on Saturdays when you two were teenagers, to take you clothes shopping, or anywhere else for that matter, until the sun was almost setting. I knew where you two would be."

"Mom, we used to take a picnic lunch and go fishin' when I was in law school, too. Not as often, though, as Brett sometimes worked with his father in construction on a Saturday. Those were the days."

Just then, Jacob walked in sleepy-eyed. He looked over at Bri and smiled. Patting the corner chair post as he sat down, he asked as if he was puzzled, "Bri, where's my cap?"

"Lucky Dog," she said with delight as she looked over at her fashion creation.

"Jacob, you're not usually up this early. What's up?"

"Oh, some friends and I are meeting in Apalachicola and going skateboarding around town and down by the city dock."

"Thought it must be something," I said, "to get you up this early."

"Who wants to butter toast," Mom asked.

I looked more awake than Jacob, so I volunteered for the task. In no time, we were all seated at the table with bacon, eggs, toast and coffee. Dad had come in from outside at just the right time, and our conversation drifted to other things.

Just as I was about to get up and go back to my bedroom to get dressed for the day, we could hear the front screen door open and a knock on the door. Mom went to answer it and then came back to the kitchen.

"Kristen, you need to see this," she said.

"What?" I said quizzically as I slowly got up and walked out to the living room and across to the front door.

As I approached the door, I looked out through the screen and saw Brett standing there. His jeans were rolled up mid calf as he stood there in his bare feet. He was holding up a large paper bag with the top folded over in one hand and a fishing pole with bait in the other. His cap was on backward.

"Sardines and crackers, ham and cheese sandwiches, and the sodas are in the cooler," he said as he raised the bag and nodded over to his vehicle. "Kristen, let's go fishin'."

I stood there and just smiled in amazement for a long time. Then, I accepted his invitation, although I let him know that I may not be able to last all day. Maybe a half day would be better.

"Perfect," Brett said as he entered my parent's bungalow to wait while I dressed and got ready.

Mom was more than willing to spend the day with Briana and cut two slices of her fresh baked apple pie for our picnic.

*****

The sky was clear and light blue as Brett packed the small drink cooler, picnic lunch sandwiches, and sardines and crackers in the bow of his small wooden john boat. He lay the fishing poles along the side and put the bait can under a seat. I slipped off my sandals and took his outstretched hand as he helped me into the boat much in the same way a prince offers his hand to help a princess into her royal coach. A year ago, I could not have imagined this, being back in this small boat with Brett idling the hours away.

Brett started the two-horsepower motor and we slowly began our excursion. Born and raised on the Cape, I loved fishing, probably more than Brett. Fishing in the river, the bay, the ocean, it didn't matter, I loved it all. By the time I was three-years-old, my father had taught me how to fillet a fish. It's like riding a bicycle; you never forget. Brett was sitting at the stern, navigating us out in the bay to our favorite fishing spot. It was never a matter of *if* we would catch fish, just *how many* and *what kind*. I loved the sound of the little motor and the feel of the gentle breeze blowing across my face as we travelled along the water. When we reached our destination, Brett cut the engine.

It was so quiet out on the bay. Occasionally, I could hear a small fish jump in the water or the sound of a distant seagull. Brett and I sat quietly together for a long time, hoping to catch a fish. I was thankful for the quiet, not wanting to talk about all that had happened the past few years, not wanting to elaborate on anything I had disclosed to him the other day, not wanting to spoil the moment. Brett's line was the first to have a bite, but the fish was small, and he threw it back. My line was next with a good size Grouper, good enough to eat for dinner. When we had fished for almost two hours and both caught a small yet respectable amount, Brett asked if I was hungry.

I turned and looked back at Brett. Nodding, I said, "Are you thinking what I'm thinking?"

"BK Islet?" he softly said with that special look in his eyes.

BK Islet is the name we gave the very small island we discovered our senior year in high school, *BK* for Brett and Kristen. We could walk around the islet in less than an hour, and it had a small clump of trees, mostly small scrub oaks, thin pines and some palms, in the center if we wanted shade for a picnic. This day the end of October, however, we could picnic on the beach.

I looked deeply into Brett's eyes. "This is one of the purest things I used to do… just come out here on a Saturday afternoon with you." I paused.

A faint smile started to form in the corners of Brett's mouth. "How many hours do you imagine we have spent whittling the time away out here?" he asked as he motioned to the vastness of bay waters and sky. His eyes glistened with that look that told me he was right where he wanted to be… with me.

I reached out my arm, took his chin in my hand, and lightly rubbed his bottom lip with my thumb. It was stillness all around, just the soft slow lapping of the bay water against the boat. Brett just kept his eyes fixated on me.

We sat there quietly, looking into one another's eyes with such intensity, until a large fish jumped out of the water by our boat and splashed down into it again.

"*BK Islet*, it is," Brett said as he secured the fishing poles, put them down on the side of the boat, started the small motor, and headed to our secret place. Whenever we set out into the bay, it was our world as if no one else could enter.

When we reached the islet, it was as beautiful as I remembered it, and no one was there. We never told anyone about the islet, but I'm sure others had discovered it as well.

We spread the blanket I had brought from home and put the sandwiches, chips, and apple pie on it. Brett got the small cooler with drinks from the bow of the boat. It was such a pleasant day, not too hot and not yet too cold even though it was almost November. We ate and made idle talk, nothing serious but light conversation that generated smiles and laughter. After we ate, Brett sat leaning up against a large palm tree near our picnic blanket. He spread out his legs in the sand and beckoned me to come and sit in front of him. I did, and his arms wrapped around me as we sat together and looked out at the water. We soon fell fast asleep listening only to the gentle rhythmic lap of the water against the boat.

After what seemed like a long afternoon nap, I awoke to the sounds of seagulls casing out what food was left on our picnic blanket. They hadn't yet converged upon it but seemed to be talking about it amongst themselves. I felt the wind, not the soft sea breeze, but wind gusts against me and looked up into the sky to see lots of dark clouds. Then, I heard low thunder. It took me only a moment to snap back into reality.

"Brett," I said urgently. "Brett, it looks like a storm is coming in."

Brett jumped up. "We better head back," he said as he quickly lifted one end of the blanket and I the other. We hurriedly got everything back in the small boat and shoved off.

The wind gusts were gaining in strength, and we could feel soft pellets of rain that were teasing out a big storm to come. The water was now choppy with little white caps. We made our way across the bay to where we had put in. Brett pulled the boat up, turned it over, and decided to come back for it later. We just made it into the safe dry vehicle when it started to fully rain.

It was only a short drive home. We could see the spindly pine trees bending like rubber, the tree tops bending and touching the sand. The last time I had seen pine trees do that was that summer when I was a teenager that we had to wait out a hurricane at home.

We pulled in our drive just in time. As we made a dash to the front porch, the sky opened up and water just poured out in a thousand pellets that beat upon us all at once – a Florida downpour. We ran for cover, it was almost as if the rain was speeding up and chasing us. Just as we climbed the steps and made it onto the front porch, the downpour completed itself and formed a curtain of rain from the tin roof overlay straight down to the sandy ground.

"You OK, Kris?" Brett asked when we'd made it onto the porch.

I just wanted to get us both inside. As I reached for the screen door, it pushed open. My mother was on the other side pushing open the door and helping us in.

"Where are your brothers?" she asked.

I looked at her quizzically, Brett by my side. "My brothers, what do you mean, Mom?"

"Your brothers," my mom said, "when we heard the severe weather warning, they went out in the bay to get you."

Eleven

There was a loud rumble coming from the sky, *Rumble... Rumble... Crackle...* then *BOOM!* My mother no sooner got her words out that my brothers had gone out in the storm to look for us and let us know about the severe weather report than lightening flashed, and a large explosion of thunder crashed.

I looked from Mom to Brett and back to Mom again.

"Do you know where they put out from?" Brett asked my mom.

"No, but Johnny keeps a boat down by the City Dock in Apalachicola. Sometimes, when the shrimp boats are late coming in, and he's waiting to load his truck, he sets out and fishes or idles his time away."

"Mom, Johnny's boat wouldn't stand up in this storm," I said with panic in my voice. "Where's Dad?"

Mom gave me a look that told me she had no idea where Dad was.

"Kris, don't worry," Brett said quite emphatically, "trust God." He cupped my face in his hands and looked seriously straight into my eyes, "Kris, trust me," he said.

Then, looking at both me and Mom, he said, "I've got a buddy that's a crew member on the U.S. Coast Guard *Seahawk* docked in Carrabelle. We'll find them." Brett no sooner got the words out than he was out the door, and I could hear the crushed oyster shells as he hurriedly backed up and pulled out of the drive."

The cutter *Seahawk* is an 87-foot marine protector class patrol boat docked in Carrabelle for small boat search and rescue. The boat has a crew of ten, one captain and nine servicemen. At least one crew member is always on duty, keeping watch, and answering the phone. The boat needs to be ready to launch should they get a call from the Panama City U.S. Coast Guard dispatch or the Franklin County Sheriff's Office. Hopefully, Brett's buddy is on call this week-end or lives on Brett's way there. We can hope and pray, at least.

"Kris," Mom said as she went to sit down by the phone, "you know how this area is. Locals are always ready to come to the rescue with their boats in addition to search and rescue." She started to dial some of the people we knew, some of the men who had bigger boats and would go out to look for them straight away.

I was exhausted. I had tried to live like a normal person today, not one that was terminally ill with cancer. I had overdone it, going out in the bay with Brett and picnicking on our small island. I settled down on the living room couch and listened as Mom made her calls. Briana must have been taking a late nap.

Time passed, and Mom and I heard nothing. The storm continued. God, please let them be OK, I silently prayed.

Rrrrring. Mom jumped to get the phone. It was Ted Simmons who had joined the search.

"Jenna," he said to Mom, "Johnny's boat he keeps down by the City Dock has gone out, but it's nowhere to be found in the bay. I saw the *Seahawk* going out into the sea."

"Out into the sea!" I heard the worry in Mom's voice. She listened for a couple minutes to what Mr. Simmons was saying and then said, "OK, thank you," and hung up.

A sleepy-eyed Briana came walking into the living room. The phone must have awakened her from her nap.

"Briana," Mom said, "tell Mommy what a good nap you had."

"Kris, she's been asleep since about two-thirty."

It crossed my mind that we may all be up late tonight, depending on what happens. Briana climbed up onto the couch with me and snuggled in my arms. I closed my eyes and thought about my brothers.

God, you wouldn't take my brothers from me, I thought. I'm the one who's dying. That would be a dirty trick. Jacob is just a young teenager.

By this time, the pounding rain had stopped, and through the open window onto the porch, you could hear the occasional drops from the roof hitting on a leaf below or the wet ground. The thunder now sounded faint in the distance. How dare the storm move away, I thought, with all the destruction it left in its wake! We still didn't know if Johnny and Jacob were safe.

Mom went into the kitchen to make us a late dinner. She cooked up the fish Brett and I had caught earlier and made some cheese grits. We ate in the living room, almost in silence, only occasional small talk with Briana, and waited on the phone to ring.

It was dusk, and, as I stood in the doorway and looked outside, it seemed so still and quiet. Only one or two crickets could be heard beginning their nightly chorus. Time seemed to pass so slowly as we waited on word of my brothers.

Just as I turned and began to walk back into the living room, I heard what sounded like the distant sound of a motor vehicle coming down the peninsula road toward our bungalow. I stood still for a moment in my tracks. The sound got louder... then I could see them as I heard the tires crushing on the oyster shell drive. It was Brett... and I saw Johnny in the front seat.

Their doors opened, and they got out as I made my way to them, Mom with Briana not far behind me. Brett made his way to me with haste. His hair was all disheveled, and his clothes had been wet and dried out some. He never looked handsomer.

"Well, *Son*," I said as I wrapped my arms around Johnny. "It's about time you came home." I was so glad to see him. Then, I looked around. Where was Jacob?

"Jacob, where's Jacob?" I asked almost frantically.

Brett put his arms around me and held me tight.

"He's going to be OK," he said. "He's going to be OK."

"OK? Where is he?"

We learned that Johnny's small boat had been swept out to sea. My brothers tried to fight it, but the storm was too strong. The waves were swelling, and they did their best to ride up and over each one. Thankfully, they were smart enough to put life jackets on at that point. Just as the *Seahawk* caught sight of them, a wave crested before they were able to pass over it. It capsized their boat, and Jacob was thrown out of it. He hit his head on something, maybe the motor, as the boat tumbled. Both Johnny and Jacob were picked up, but Jacob was flown by medevac to a hospital in Panama City. "Just as a precaution," Brett said.

I looked at Johnny. "And your boat?"

"Looks like I'll need another one," he said with a chuckle.

"Now *Son*," I said and smiled.

"Mom," Johnny said sounding more serious, "I think we should all drive over to Panama City and see how Jacob is doing."

We all agreed, drove the hour or so over, and found Jacob in the emergency room doing fine… but a little shook up. They wanted to keep him overnight for observation since he had hit his head.

"Kristen, you wouldn't believe it," Jacob said as he sat up straighter in his hospital bed, his eyes as big as saucers. "We were out in the bay looking for you when the current just swept us out to sea. All of a sudden, the dark waves were bigger than mountains and the rain was pulsating down. The wind blew the rain in all directions. I almost couldn't even see Johnny, but we could hear each other as we yelled over the sound of the storm. We were being tossed all about in Johnny's little boat."

I couldn't help but make the parallel with my life lately. I felt like I had been tossed all about and didn't have any control. I could only imagine how frightened Jacob must have been out there in the storm, and Johnny, too, for that matter.

Mom stayed the night at the hospital with Jacob, Johnny went home with his wife Angie who met us at the hospital, and we drove back to the Cape, planning to return tomorrow.

Finally, back on the Cape after such a long day, Brett carried a sleeping Briana into her bed. I covered her up, and we both just stood and looked at her for a few minutes. She was so innocent and had no idea of what had transpired today.

Brett took my hand and led me out into the living room.

"Do you have a Bible handy?" he asked.

"Yes," I said, as I walked back to my bedroom and retrieved the Bible I kept on my bedside table.

Sitting beside me on the sofa, he opened it up and read from Matthew 8:23-26.

Then he got into the boat and his disciples followed him.
Without warning, a furious storm came
up on the lake, so that the waves
swept over the boat. But Jesus was sleeping.
The disciples went and woke him, saying,
"Lord, save us! We're going to drown!"
He replied, "You of little faith, why are you so afraid?"
Then he got up and rebuked the winds and the waves,
And it was completely calm.

"See Kris," he said as he looked into my eyes, "we didn't need to be afraid. God is in control. In the storms of life, God is with us."

Twelve

The next morning, I awoke to find Jacob getting ready for school. He had been discharged from the hospital in the early morning hours, and Mom had dropped him off to change clothes and catch the school bus. Briana's little bed was empty and her little backpack for daycare gone. I must have needed the sleep and slept like a rock. I actually felt pretty good on this morning after all the excitement of the day before.

How I felt physically seemed to go in cycles like my treatment. I had finished my third cycle of chemotherapy and had an appointment scheduled with Dr. Kerns for tomorrow. Today, I was feeling so well that I was optimistic that I would get good news when he reviewed new MRI results.

I mentally reviewed my list of things I wanted to get done when I had the energy. First on the list was to see the county prosecutor. Although Cape San Blas was in Gulf County, and the county seat was in Port St. Joe, the rape had happened in Apalachicola which was Franklin County. The peninsula of Cape San Blas is on the edge of Gulf County but almost halfway in between Port St. Joe and Apalachicola. Most of what I did in life centered in Apalachicola. My brothers and I had even been given special permission to attend school there as our mother worked for Franklin County Public Schools, in the early years as a secretary and later as a teacher, and

RETURN TO CAPE SAN BLAS

our father was an oysterman from there. We didn't go to Port St. Joe much, and I was thankful that I could go to Apalachicola where I was more familiar. Another thing I had thought of in regard to this was getting a paternity test on Briana.

Better not push my luck, I thought, and skipped taking a shower. There was the possibility that it may take all of my energy. I also decided to skip the wig at this point. Everyone I cared about had already seen me without it, and, who knew, maybe I'd get faster service with a bald head... anything to conserve energy. I went for the earrings, though, little sea green glass marble balls on 14-caret gold wires to match my sea green sweater. At least I could look somewhat feminine.

I wondered where to go to get a paternity test for Briana.

Before I came back to the Cape, I had turned in my leased Volvo coupe and then taken the Greyhound bus home. I no longer owned a car. I looked outside. Both Mom and Dad's vehicles were gone. All that was home was the camper that was parked down by Dad's workshop. Mom didn't like me driving anyway because of all the medications I was on. She was afraid that I might wreck the vehicle and get hurt or worse yet get killed in an accident. How much worse could it be? I thought. My cancer was, after all, considered terminal.

Carly, that's it, I thought as I went to the kitchen counter and dialed her number. Carly had graduated with a master's degree in marketing and worked for a company out of Panama City. Her traveling schedule was somewhat predetermined by her and flexible. Maybe Carly could pick me up.

"Carly Stephens," she answered.

"Carly, it's Kris. Is there anyway you'd have some free time today to take me into Apalach to see the county prosecutor? I'd like to get started on pressing charges against Billy Ray."

"Sure, I just have one appointment I can move around and then pick you up in about an hour. Will that do?"

73

"Perfect," I said. "See you then."

Then, I called my old family doctor's office to find out about getting a paternity test. I talked with one of Dr. Connelly's nurses and was told that I could bring Briana in and get a DNA sample taken to send to the lab with a sample from the father. I didn't need an appointment. I explained that I would be coming in later this morning with Briana, and that the man who would be tested would be in on another day.

Things seemed to be progressing, I thought. It would be good to get things resolved.

Carly arrived less than an hour after I had talked with her. I was ready to go when she pulled in the drive. It felt good to be palling around with her again.

"First stop, the court house?" Carly asked.

"Actually, no." I told Carly about my call to Dr. Connelly's office. "I want to pick up Bri at the preschool and take her to his office to get a simple swab test *on the way to have lunch at the pizzeria*. I don't want to make a big deal out of it, but I want to get it started."

"Sounds like a plan," Carly said.

Briana was very excited that Mommy and Carly had come to take her to lunch with them for pizza. Her chest swelled up with pride as she was on her way out the front door of the preschool. She told any and all little children she saw on her way out where she was going.

The stop at the doctor's office went smoothly. I made a new-patient appointment for Briana while I was there, so we'd have a doctor on call for her if she should get sick. It didn't look like we would be going back to Tampa. The swab test just seemed like a routine well child visit to her.

It was nice to have pizza again at the Market Street Pizzeria. Briana loved it and soaked up all the attention she could get sitting in the booth next to Mommy. Everyone commented on how cute she was and how much she looked like me.

When we took her back to the preschool, I told her that Mommy had other errands to run with Carly and maybe we would have pizza out again for lunch on another day. This seemed enough to satisfy her as we walked in quietly so as not to wake the other children during nap time.

It was already one o'clock in the afternoon.

As Carly and I walked up the steps of the court house, I hoped we would be able to see the county prosecutor today. We didn't have an appointment, but hopefully he would be in and have time to talk with me. As we entered the court house, we asked a woman who looked like a clerk where we would find the county prosecutor's office. She gave us directions to the Annex.

As we entered the office with the county prosecutor's name on the door, we could see past the receptionist room to an office where a middle-aged bald-headed man sat at a desk. We had part of it conquered, I thought – he was in.

I noticed the name on the receptionist's desk – Sue Ella James. "Miss James," I said as we approached her desk. "I'd like to see Mr. Kincaid if he's available."

She looked from me to Carly and back again. "Do you have an appointment?"

"No," I answered, "but we were hoping that we'd be able to see him. It's about a rape."

Mr. Kincaid had overheard our conversation and got up from behind his desk and said, "Miss James, it's OK. I'll be able to see them."

As we entered his office, Mr. Kincaid made his way toward us and extended his right hand. "Tom," he said, "Just call me Tom. How may I help you?"

"My name is Kristen Parker, and this is my friend Carly Stephens. I want to talk with you about the possibility of pressing charges against someone for rape."

Mr. Kincaid, Tom, went back and sat down behind his desk as he motioned for us to have a seat in the two empty old leather Wingback chairs. He picked up a pen and writing tablet and pushed his chair back. He bent his right leg and rested his right foot on his left knee, putting his tablet in position over his man-made desk.

"Miss Parker, when did this rape happen?"

"It was January 4th, 1999."

Mr. Kincaid, Tom, lowered his pen to rest on the tablet as he looked up at me quizzically. "January 4th, 1999? That's almost three years ago. Why are you just now reporting it?"

"I just came back to the Cape from Tampa. I left on that very night because of it. It took me this long to get up the courage to face it and come to you."

"Miss Parker, did you seek medical treatment on that night?" he asked.

"No, I was so traumatized I just left. I didn't know where I was going at the time, but I ended up in Tampa."

"Did you tell anyone?"

"No, not until recently after I came home."

"Miss Parker, do you have the clothes you wore that night, as they were, not laundered?"

"No." I could see where he was going with this. I had been in law school; how stupid could I be? He was determining if I had a case. I had checked the statute of limitations but had not thought about the implications of waiting so long.

"Miss Parker, do you have anything other than your word against his? Did anyone see you that night at the place where this happened?"

"No," I said, and began to have a queasy feeling in my stomach. "Mr. Kincaid, he assaulted me and raped me and then threatened me!"

"Miss Parker, I am so sorry. What was his threat?"

"He told me he would send me home in a box if I told anyone."

Carly, who had been sitting quietly in the chair by my side, turned to Mr. Kincaid and spoke up for me. "Mr. Kincaid, Kristen has been living in fear ever since this rape. It caused her to flee from the only home she knew. It took my friend away. She has been living in bondage to this now for almost three years. And what about him, the man who did this to her, Billy Ray, what about him?"

Mr. Kincaid showed a sign of recognition when Carly mentioned Billy Ray's name, and rightly so. Everyone within a fifty-mile radius knew Billy Ray's reputation.

"Billy Ray, is that Billy Ray Sorles?" he asked as he looked in my direction.

"Yes, Mr. Kincaid, it is."

Mr. Kincaid sat there quietly for a moment as if he was pondering what he could do. Then, he spoke, "Miss Parker, I am so sorry. I wish I could help you, but I just don't see that we have a case. It would just be your word against his, and the jury would wonder why you waited so long to report this."

I gave a long breath-full sigh and then asked, "Then what am I supposed to do?"

Mr. Kincaid looked genuinely sorry and defeated, defeated before we had even started a case, and said. "Miss Parker, maybe just try to forget it, and if he ever does bother you again, come to me immediately so I can help you."

I looked at him. Just try to forget it? Obviously, he knew nothing about being raped, but I knew he was right about not having a case. Yes, I could press charges, but the chances of winning were slim to none, and then how would I feel if we lost? Carly and I rose from our chairs and thanked him for his time. All I could say was that yes, I would contact him right away if anything ever did happen again.

When we got back to Carly's car and I slipped into the front passenger seat, tears welled up in my eyes. "What now, Carly, what now?"

She leaned over from the driver's seat and put her arms around me. "We'll think of something. Just give me time."

I decided to put all that we had started today on hold until we figured out if there was anything else we could do. I would think about it later, but no more today. I was tired, and for now, I decided, maybe I needed to give it to God. I remembered a Bible verse, Isaiah 55:8-9 – *"For my thoughts are not your thoughts, neither are your ways my ways," declares the Lord. "As the heavens are higher than the earth, so are my ways higher than your ways and my thoughts than your thoughts."* Maybe that's what I needed, a way that only God could think of.

We rode in silence for a short time, and then Carly asked, "Kristen, did you ever tell your mother about seeing your dad with Viola Peters?"

"No, but today is probably as good a day as any, a perfect ending to a perfectly terrible day."

"Now Kristen, the whole day wasn't terrible. We had lunch with Briana at the pizzeria."

She was right, of course, but I felt like all that I had attempted was in vain, a perfect waste of a day, and who knew how many days I had left. When we got home, I thanked Carly for picking me up and spending most of the day with me. She really was a lot of support.

"Good luck with your mom," she said as she pulled out of the drive.

It was almost three o'clock when I got home, so I had time to take a short nap before Mom would arrive. I awoke when I heard the crushing of tires on the oyster shell drive. I lifted myself from where I had been lying on the sofa and looked out the front window. It was Mom.

As she entered through the back kitchen screen door with a small bag of groceries, I got up and went into the kitchen to meet her. Seems like Mom went to the grocery store almost every day on her way home from work.

"Hi Mom, what are we having for dinner tonight?" I asked as I peeked into the bag.

"I thought we'd have Granny's famous hamburg stroganoff," she said as she got out that old rusted recipe box, put it on the counter, tilted the lid up, and lifted the recipe so she could read it and leave it in place.

"Umm yum," I responded. Granny, my mom's mom, had passed away when I was just a teenager. She always made me feel like I was her favorite, and I missed her greatly. Mom said though that we would all see her again one day in heaven, and this seemed to have given me some comfort at the time.

"Do you want me to cut up some onions," I asked.

"Sure, and the recipe also calls for a clove of garlic minced if you want to add that."

I walked over to the counter and retrieved the cutting board, a sharp knife from the rack, and took the garlic and enough onions from the grocery bag to make a cup chopped. My stamina didn't seem to last long since I had started chemotherapy treatments, and I had already used my quota for the day, so I headed to take my place in a chair at the table.

"Mom," I said as I began cutting an end off an onion, "there's something I've been needing to talk with you about, but I'm not sure how to say it." Mom had gotten the large frying pan out and was looking for the small can of mushrooms to brown in butter with the onions and garlic.

"Well, honesty's the best policy," she said. "Maybe just start at the beginning."

"That's just it, Mom. I don't think Dad's being honest with you." With that, Mom stopped what she was doing, turned, and looked startlingly over at me.

"What do you mean?" she asked. "What are you talking about?"

"Well, I don't know what this means, but the other day when Carly and I were leaving the Market Street Pizzeria, we saw Dad and Viola Peters leaving the River Oasis together."

"Kristen, Dad does frequent the River Oasis from time to time. You know he doesn't drink beer any longer like he used to, but he goes there sometimes to talk with his buddies, other fishermen."

"Mom, we followed them, and they went into the Riverfront Inn. She was hanging all over Dad and they were very engrossed in what they were talking about on the way over and seemed intent on where they were going."

Mom just stood there. I wondered if the preheating pan was going to burn.

Then, she finally spoke. "You know, I sometimes wonder when Dad goes off to work on these projects of his if that's what he's really doing. I've had this uneasy feeling, but I haven't had anything I could pinpoint. Viola Peters? Of all people!" she exclaimed as she began to cry.

I thought of my parents. When did Mom and Dad meet? The question may more aptly be asked – when did they not know one another? Mom grew up on the Cape and Dad grew up in Apalachicola, the son of a commercial fisherman. They met when Mom was in fifth grade and Dad was in sixth. Dad was so enthralled with the girls that year that he failed sixth grade, hence they were in the same grade forevermore through middle and high school. And Mom… she helped Dad with all of his business endeavors. When he was oysterin', she would shuck; when he was fishin', she would clean fish, when he would buy a dilapidated house, she would help him renovate it. She didn't go back to school to further her education and become a teacher until after the oysterin' business slowed and Dad began escaping to this or that "project" that he supposedly did by himself.

"I know, I thought of that too. Viola Peters of all people."

"Well, I'm not sure what I'm going to do."

"Maybe we should follow him sometime, you, me, Carly and Leigh. We could tag team him, and he wouldn't realize we were following him."

"That's a thought."

Just then, Dad came in with Briana from preschool.

Thirteen

It was November 21, 2001, and I had finished my third cycle of chemotherapy. I was on my way to see Dr. Kerns to learn if I was winning my battle with cancer. Brett had offered to take off work and drive me to the Cancer Center. When we got in his vehicle and he put his hands on the steering wheel as we backed out of the drive, I noticed his right hand was black and blue and swollen.

"Brett, what did you do to your hand?" I asked with a slightly raised voice.

"Oh, nothing. I just hurt it the other day."

"Hurt it? How?"

Brett was quiet for a moment and then said, "Just something I had to take care of."

When he said that, I knew. "Brett, you didn't…?"

Again, Brett was quiet for a moment, and then he responded very adamantly, "Yes, I did."

Brett reached over and turned on some music. I really didn't want to have a conversation about Billy Ray and the rape, so for most of the way we traveled in silence, just listening to the music.

When we got close to the Cancer Center, I told Brett that I was feeling much better since I had finished my third cycle of chemo and was hoping for a good report.

"Whatever we need to do, Kris, we will do to fight this cancer."

Brett pulled up in front of the Center and we got out, letting the valet workers park his vehicle. I thought how it was a shame that there was so much cancer that the Center looked like Grand Central Station and needed to have valet parking to accommodate all the patients who came and went.

We entered the large lobby on the main floor and made our way to the lab to get blood work done and radiology to have an MRI – it would be a long day. Then, we took the elevator up to the Thoracic Clinic and Dr. Kerns' office. As we entered the waiting room, I saw Mom sitting there watching the door for me. She had taken a few hours off from work to meet us there and find out what the doctor had to say about my progress.

"Hi, Kristen, Brett."

"Hey, Mom," I said as I slid onto the couch next to the chair she was sitting in. Brett sat down right beside me and rested his arm on the back of the couch behind me.

The TV at the far end of the waiting room was still reporting on the aftermath of 9/11. Mom had elected not to sit down at that end. As much as we felt for the families of the victims of the attacks, none of us could seem to concentrate on any of it since my diagnosis on that same day.

A small kitchen cabinet unit in the corner was equipped with coffee and juice. Juice seemed to be a big thing at the Center, probably to give us energy to help us make the effort it took just to come and go to our doctors' appointments and treatments.

"Do you want something to drink?" Brett asked me right after we'd sat down and then lifted his head to Mom.

"Maybe some coffee," I responded.

"No thank you," Mom said. "I'm fine."

Brett got up and fixed us both a cup of coffee. It was strange, but since I'd been back, I hadn't had to remind him of how I took it. It was as if I'd never left. He even knew what to order as a drink for me if I was in the restroom at a restaurant when the waitress came. Coffee, lattes, no matter, he remembered.

The waiting room was full, and it seemed like we had to wait a long time. The atmosphere was sad and pleasant at the same time. People seemed nicer when they had cancer. They didn't seem to sweat the petty stuff and were nice to one another. The people who worked at the Center seemed to do everything they could to make your day as pleasant as it could be under the circumstances.

We were finally called. "Kristen Parker," a nurse called out as she leaned against the opened door to the treatment area. At least at this Center, I had a name. I wasn't number 10 or 3 or 103. Not only did I have a name, but every time I went to the Center, I was issued a wristband with my name on it, and it was checked numerous times during my visit. We all got up and paraded in, Brett and Mom behind me, anxious to find out what Dr. Kerns would say.

The first thing the nurse always did was weigh me and take my blood pressure in the little nook in the hall before she escorted me to a room. The rooms all looked the same – an examination table with a curtain that could be pulled around it, a small desk with a computer and phone, one stool for the doctor and two chairs on the other side of the desk, one for the patient and one for the family member or friend who came with them. There was also a screen to read X-rays, etc. and a box of tissues. Always a box of tissues, didn't look good, but hopefully I was going to be one of the lucky ones today and told my treatments had worked and that I had beat this cancer.

As the nurse ushered us into a room, she went and got an extra chair as I had both Brett and Mom with me today. We waited anxiously. Within the hour, this doctor's words could change my whole life... or end it.

Dr. Kerns came in with a smile. He was such a professional looking kind man. I wondered how he could do this job year in and year out. He greeted us and motioned for me to hop up on the examining table that was in a sitting position. I was glad to finally be done with the third cycle of my chemotherapy treatments and getting the results. I so much wanted to be rid of this cancer.

"Kristen, how have you been feeling?" Dr. Kerns asked. "How have you been tolerating the treatments?"

"Actually, I've been feeling much better the last couple of days although I've been very fatigued, very tired."

"She had a rough time through the treatments," my mom added. "Sometimes, she was very sick, very sick, and had to stay in bed."

"That's to be expected," Dr. Kerns responded. "She has been on some heavy-duty chemotherapy drugs."

I was anxiously awaiting the results of having taken those drugs. I hung on every word, waiting for his new prognosis.

"Kristen, the tumors are shrinking, but they're not all gone. The treatments have helped but have not eradicated your cancer."

What does that mean? I wanted to scream. Am I going to live? Can I beat this cancer with another treatment… or am I going to die?

"So, what do we do now?" I asked. "Try another chemotherapy drug?"

"Whoa," Dr. Kerns said, "I think you need to have a break from chemotherapy. Your body needs a rest, and you need time to recover from all the treatments you've had. Now that the tumors have shrunk, and there has been an improvement, take some time to enjoy life. Get out and have some fun."

Brett looked at me and smiled. "I can take care of that, Dr. Kerns."

Mom sat quietly as if she was contemplating whether it was time to ask her next question. "Dr. Kerns, Kristen has small cell cancer, and I believe you said the main site is her lungs. Could I give her one of my lungs that is cancer free to replace her lungs that have cancer? Could we both live with one cancer free lung?"

Dr. Kerns gave a small smile that Mom had asked the question. I think he had probably been asked that question before with other patients. Then, he got serious and explained that my cancer had already spread throughout my body.

He looked at Mom and continued, "Kristen's cancer spread before we even knew she had cancer and manifested as a lump in her breast, which is rare in the first place that it would manifest in soft tissue like the breast. We already know that it has spread to her spine that her back pain alerted us to. Having a lung transplant would not solve her problem; it would not cure her. Her cancer cannot be cured with surgery."

The more Dr. Kerns explained, the graver it sounded. He turned to me and said, "Kristen, we are going to continue to fight this and give you as much time as we can. We are not giving up, but I want you to know the nature of the cancer you have. It is very aggressive and has already spread."

What could I say after that?

He continued, "Kristen, your red blood cell count is low, and you said you have been feeling very fatigued and tired. I want you to go over to the Infusion Center and receive some blood today. I think it will make you feel better."

Again, what could I say? We set a date for me to come back, and Dr. Kerns gave me orders to go home and enjoy the Thanksgiving and Christmas holidays. Mom, Brett, and I all walked out rather quietly. Mom gave me a hug when we got outside and then went back to work. Brett and I headed across the street to the Infusion Center.

When we walked in to the Infusion Center, I was surprised that there was almost no one there. Maybe it was because it was so late in the day just before the holidays. There was a little boy across the room from where the nurse took me and Brett. He looked to be about nine or ten.

"I'm April, and I'll be your nurse today," a young woman said. Dr. Kerns just called your order in, so it will be a few minutes to get what we need for you. You can have a seat and make yourselves comfortable." As if I could get comfortable here. Who was she kidding?

"Thanks," Brett responded.

We sat quietly at first, and Brett reached over and took my hand. He was here, I thought. He hadn't run. Maybe he did truly love me.

I looked across the room at the little bald-headed boy who was with his father and wondered what kind of cancer he had. I thought how cancer did not discriminate based on age and wondered what his prognosis was. Although the father and son were talking softly, we could clearly hear what they were saying as there was no one else in the room.

The father was holding a glove in his hand, and he told his son that his hand was his spirit and the glove was his body. He explained to the little boy that his spirit existed before birth. As he slipped his hand into the glove, he told his son that his spirit came to live in his body when he was born to his mother and father. When he explained that the spirit lives after death, he slowly slipped his hand out of the glove.

I looked at that rumpled glove lying there on the father's lap after he told his story. I felt like my spirit, the real me, may be in my body, but my body had taken on a life of its own these past few years. I had been keeping busy but not living. I vowed to slow down and make each moment count. I vowed to give Briana as much of me as I could for as long as I had with her.

After about twenty minutes, the nurse came with my first unit of blood. I would have two. Just when we were sure that we would be the only ones at the Infusion Center on this day before Thanksgiving, with the exception of the young boy and his father, Abby came in the door.

She looked frail and peaked, almost to the point of emaciation. Although Abby had a different type of cancer, Stage IV non-Hodgkin's lymphoma, we sometimes experienced the same symptoms. At times, she would have pain or shortness of breath from the pressure of her enlarged lymph nodes on her respiratory organs. The chemotherapy made her nauseated, and she didn't eat well. Abby was a beautiful thin and lanky young woman when she was healthy. When she lost her appetite, she became so thin that I wondered how long she could make it. Her beautiful blue eyes sunk back into her face when she wasn't feeling well, and her shoulder and upper arm bones protruded through the thin pull-over sweaters she wore.

Abby didn't always have the encouragement at home to eat. When I was extremely sick from my chemotherapy, Mom would make me egg custard or go out and get me chocolate ice cream. She always had dinner on the table and had items on the menu that she thought I could easily tolerate – macaroni and cheese and mashed potatoes. My oldest brother Johnny would stop by and make us peanut butter and marshmallow fluff sandwiches, a favorite from our childhood days. How could I resist at least taking a few bites when he came all the way down to the Cape after work, rather than going home, to coax me to eat? My youngest brother Jacob would fix us both a snack when he came home from school.

Abby, on the other hand, had lost her mother to breast cancer when she was still a young girl. Her parents had divorced before she was old enough to even know what divorce was. When her mother and father divorced, they parted ways, and Abby and her older brother hadn't the first clue where to find their father. Abby was eleven and her brother eighteen when their mother died. James, her older brother, had been working constructing and repairing shrimp nets since he was old enough to work part-time. It was a very valued skill in Franklin County, and he was able to continue making the mortgage payments on the small house their mother left them in Eastpoint. Just the two of them against the world.

They had managed rather well until Abby's diagnosis of non-Hodgkin's lymphoma. When Abby became an adult, they both remained living as friends and housemates in the same house their mother had left them. They both led independent lives but were there for one another when needed. When Abby or her brother had a cold or the flu, the other one would bring home medicine. Abby would sometimes make homemade chicken noodle soup for her brother when he was sick. They also kept an eye on one another's dates through the years to make sure their brother or sister was being treated right. Cancer, though, was different. The uncertainty of her prognosis was hard for James to deal with. When she was too sick to drive herself to treatments, James drove her, but he unintentionally seemed to emotionally distance himself from the disease. He spent more and more of his time at the shop making and repairing nets.

"Hey Abby," I said as she took a seat in the recliner directly across from us. "I didn't expect to see you here today."

"Dr. Clayton is adding rituximab to my CHOP chemotherapy and wanted me to get a treatment in before the holiday. Now, I'm on R-CHOP. The rituximab is supposed to improve the outcome of the other chemotherapy drugs in CHOP. Think I've got you beat for a long time," she said smiling. "What are you doing here? I thought you finished your third cycle of the chemotherapy the other day and were doing better."

"Oh, I did, but I've been feeling fatigued and tired lately. I just had a follow-up visit with Dr. Kerns, and he sent me over to get a couple units of blood. I think he wants to make sure I have plenty of red blood cell energy for the holidays."

I turned to look at Brett and asked, "Hon, I'm feeling kind of hungry. Do you think you could go get us something to eat?"

"Sure, do you want something from the cafeteria at the Center across the street, or do you want me to go through a drive-thru?"

"Do you mind going across the street?" I was actually thinking maybe I could help Abby get some calories in during our visit.

"You got it. What do you want me to get?"

I looked over at Abby and asked her if she'd like something from across the street, our treat. At first, she didn't seem very interested, but then I reminded her about the deliciously extravagant chocolate peanut butter pie they had. I was thinking that the peanut butter would be healthy at the same time.

"OK, you sold me, a slice of peanut butter pie and a milk."

Brett looked over my way and asked, "What about you?"

"I'll have whatever looks good for dinner *and* the chocolate peanut butter pie and milk."

"Got it," he said as he rose from his chair and made his way across the room to the door.

April came over and got Abby started. It always struck me how matter-of-fact everything was done at the Infusion Center, just like it was nothing out of the ordinary, a pit stop in our day.

When Brett had left, Abby asked, "Kristen, did you start the process yet to press charges against Billy Ray for rape?" She remembered our conversation after I had brought it up with the social worker.

"Actually, I tried. I went to the county prosecutor's office in Apalachicola, but he doesn't think I have a case. When I left the Cape that night, I didn't tell anyone what happened, and I didn't go to the hospital for evidence. He said it's just my word against his. I know he's right, but it just doesn't seem fair."

Abby looked down at the floor in a kind of wide-eyed stare.

After a couple of moments, I continued. "I've decided to give it to God, at least for the time being. I don't know what to do next, but maybe He does."

Abby made a kind of clicking noise, pulling air in her mouth as she smacked her tongue against its roof, shook her head gently from left to right, and then let out a deep sigh. I could tell she genuinely felt bad for me.

"You know," I said, "I've been thinking about some Bible stories I learned when I was a kid. You know, the one in 2 Chronicles where a vast army was against Jehoshaphat and he didn't have the power to face them and win. He didn't know what to do, so he prayed to God, and God fought the battle for him. The Lord said the battle wasn't his, Jehoshaphat's, but God's. Maybe God has a plan that I don't know about."

Abby was unusually quiet but answered, "Maybe so."

"What brother of Billy Ray's did you date? I asked her.

"Buddy Lee."

Just then, Brett appeared with lots of goodies. "What have we here?" I asked.

"Beef tips over noodles with kale and corn," he said as he began taking clear plastic containers out of a large bag. "Abby, I brought plenty if you'd like some… and walla, chocolate peanut butter pie and milk, sweet tea for me."

I needed to give Brett a lot of credit. He remembered how much I liked southern cooked kale, and the beef tips over noodles looked and smelled delicious. Abby said she would take a little, but just a little, of the dinner. It was amazing how much we enjoyed our dinner together considering where we were and why we were there.

"So, Abby," I asked, "what are your plans for Thanksgiving tomorrow?"

"Oh, I haven't really made any."

"Why don't you come to our house? Brett will be there," I said as I motioned his way, "and my friend Carly and my mom's friend Leigh, and you could meet Briana. My oldest brother Johnny will be there with his wife, Angie, and I have another younger brother Jacob. Oh, and my cousin Rebecca is coming with her husband and son."

"I'd love to, but I'm not sure. My brother James may be planning on having Thanksgiving dinner with me."

"You could bring him," I said. "The invitation's open for both of you."

Abby lit up and said, "I think I will ask him."

"Let me give you directions to my house." I got out my pen and a piece of paper from my purse and drew a small map with directions to our home on the Cape. I really hoped she'd come.

Fourteen

I awoke the next morning feeling so good I wondered if I even had cancer at all. Maybe it had all been a mistake. Just wishful thinking, but maybe I was getting better. Even Dr. Kerns, with his extensive degrees in the field of medical science, admitted that only God knows the number of days in my life. Maybe I'm not going to die early. Maybe I'm going to die right when God planned. Maybe my life will be exactly as long as it's supposed to be.

I glanced at the clock on my bedside table. I had slept in till almost nine o'clock. We had a tradition in our family not to wake up on Thanksgiving morning until we just naturally woke up. Other people got up before the crack of dawn to stuff their turkeys and make pies. Not us, we got up whenever we happened to and started making stuffing and preparing the turkey after breakfast. Thanksgiving dinner was timed to be however many hours the wrapper on the fresh Butterball turkey said we needed to cook it, after we got it in the oven. Usually, that meant about two or three o'clock in the afternoon.

Mom had made two homemade pecan pies from the recipe in Granny's old rusted recipe box and then baked two Mrs. Smith's pumpkin custard pies the night before. Those were Dad's favorites – pecan and pumpkin. Leigh was always watching her weight and was going to bring her specialty, a no-sugar low-cal fruit pie she made in a graham cracker crust with pineapple on the bottom, then bananas, then berries and no-sugar low-fat vanilla pudding on the top. Carly, of course, brought wine, and lots of it.

As I pulled back the covers and got out of bed, I noticed the slight breeze blowing in through the southwest bedroom window I had left cracked the night before. It was a little chilly but perfect for Thanksgiving Day. It would warm up later as the sun rose in the sky.

"Lucky Dog wants a biscuit," I could faintly hear my little daughter telling her grandmother in the kitchen.

"You can give him one," I heard my mom reply. "They're on top of his food tub over there in the corner."

I heard a little shriek of glee and could picture Lucky intently following her, waiting on his treat.

I threw on my long bathrobe and headed for the kitchen. I could smell Mom's homemade sweet rolls or braided coffee ring in the oven. Whichever one she had made smelled just about ready to come out.

When I entered the kitchen, I was surprised to see Brett sitting there at the kitchen table.

"Good Morning," I said with a yawn. "Brett, what are you doing here so early?"

"Oh, I just thought I'd come over and take Little Miss Briana out for breakfast, so you and your mom can start Thanksgiving dinner."

"Briana, would you like to go out to breakfast with Brett this morning?"

"I need shoes," she said as she toddled to our bedroom.

"Guess she would," I said with a smile.

Briana came out with two little slip-on shoes. "Better wear your sneakers with socks," I said. "It's a little chilly outside this morning."

After I put Briana's shoes on, Dad came in from outside, and Mom put the sweet rolls on the table.

"Briana, let's have a sweet roll before we leave," Brett said as he got up to pour himself a second cup of coffee from the coffee maker on the counter. Dad also poured himself a cup, and we all sat down and dug into the rolls. I loved holding a roll in my left hand and slowly pulling it apart, little by little, to eat with my fingers.

As it was a holiday, Jacob would probably sleep until just before the dinner was ready. "Johnny's on his way over," Mom said, "to help set up for the dinner. If your friend Abby and her brother come, we'll have fifteen. I thought we could put all the picnic tables together and eat outside in the back. I have those gold tablecloths and the fall holiday foliage we can put around. I also bought some extra Adirondack chairs last summer that are down in the garage."

After we leisurely sat at the kitchen table and ate sweet rolls, Mom got up to start making the stuffing. She had been simmering the giblets since earlier when she got up.

"Let me get dressed," I said, "and I'll start cutting up the celery and sage for the stuffing."

Mom got out a large glass mixing bowl and emptied two bags of seasoned stuffing cubes. She used the broth from simmering the giblets and melted the required amount of butter in it. Then, she got out the turkey and started getting it ready.

It didn't take us long working together to get the stuffing made and into the turkey. Then, we started working on the sweet potato casserole. We always had lots of starches on Thanksgiving – stuffing, sweet potato casserole, and lots of mashed potatoes. Mom made two kinds. One was just regular homemade mashed potatoes. The other had small baby cooked carrots whipped in just lightly so they were still small pieces. That's the way my brother Jacob liked them.

"What about rolls?" I asked my mom.

"Angie's bringing homemade yeast rolls, and she made a pumpkin roll she saw an easy recipe for in a magazine."

"Think we've got it covered," I said.

It wasn't long before Johnny arrived, and he and Dad started setting up the tables. We had a large brick grill in the backyard that Dad had made years ago. I asked him if we could maybe start a fire later in the day about five when the sun started setting and it got cooler. "We could roast marshmallows over the grill," I said. "Briana loved it back when we had our oyster roast."

"Possibly," Dad replied.

Johnny helped me put the four large gold tablecloths along our newly formed long table. Then, he got the fall box out of the garage, and I got to decorate with the red, orange, and gold foliage.

"Johnny, there's some gold candles in turkey holders in the cabinet over the frig. Could you get them down for me?"

"Sure," he responded and was off to the kitchen. He also took down the large turkey platter and turkey gravy serving container with matching spoon. Everything was fall colors or turkey themed.

As I stood back and surveyed the table with arms folded across my chest, I asked, "What are we missing?"

"Follow me," Johnny said as he led the way to his pickup truck in our drive.

As we walked around to the back of his truck, I caught a glimpse of pumpkins, lots of them, filling the truck bed. There were many big ones that could line the back steps going up to the kitchen, and some small ones for table decoration.

"*Son*, you've thought of everything."

I decided to wait until later in the day to set the tables with the plates, glasses, and silverware. Johnny left and went home to be with Angie until it was time to come back for our feast. Dad disappeared to his workshop, and Brett called and asked if he could take Briana to the park after breakfast. In the meantime, Mom and I got out the teacups and made a pot of tea. All seemed right with the world.

When the turkey was done, and we slipped the last-minute green bean casserole in the oven, Carly and then Leigh arrived. Brett came through the kitchen door a moment later holding a sleeping Bri with his left arm, her head on his shoulder. With his right arm, he brought his right index finger to his lips making a quiet *shhhh…* sound. I got up and led him in to her bed, lifting her blankie to cover her with after he laid her down. We quietly tiptoed back out to the kitchen.

"She played her heart out at the park," Brett said. "I didn't think you'd mind how long we stayed."

"No, actually Mom and I have enjoyed having tea and having time to sit down and talk. Thanks for thinking of it."

There was a knock at the front door and then I heard the door open. My cousin Rebecca was coming in with her husband who was carrying another turkey with stuffing she had cooked. She also brought Granny's baked onion casserole. Her son followed with a bag full of candy corn. I wondered if we had room for all this food.

By the time we had all set the tables outside, Jacob had awakened for the morning and stumbled into the kitchen wearing jeans and barefooted. Briana woke up from her nap and came running out into the kitchen. It was a good thing we had one of those very big country eat-in kitchens. It seemed to be the hub of all we were doing today. Dad walked up from his workshop, and as the last dish of food was set on the table, all our guests had arrived except for Abby and her brother James.

Just as we were sitting down, an unfamiliar pick-up truck pulled up. We wondered who it was until the passenger door swung open, and out popped Abby. She was carrying a small serving bowl that we later discovered was Waldorf fruit salad. A good-looking dark-haired man of about 40 with dark facial hair came around from the driver's side. He looked kind of lost, not knowing anyone. I ran to greet Abby and wrapped my arms around her. "I'm so glad you could come," I said.

"This is my brother James."

I reached out to shake his hand. "We're just sitting down," I said as I led the way and introduced Abby and James to our other guests.

"Dr. Walker!" Abby exclaimed when she recognized my cousin Rebecca. As it turned out, Rebecca was her doctor at the Cancer Center. And James and Dad knew each other from their trade.

I looked around the table and couldn't believe how many people had gathered with us for Thanksgiving. We all joined hands and Dad began saying the grace. Then, as was our tradition, we went around the table and all said something we were thankful for. In addition to the family and friends I loved who were gathered with us for this feast, I was inwardly thankful that I was still alive and at home on the Cape.

Brett, who was sitting beside me, offered thanks "for Kristen being home" as he squeezed my hand, and Briana thanked God for the park. Abby gave thanks for her "new friend," and her brother offered thanks for a good business this year. When we finished the circle of thanks, everyone was ready to dig in and conversation was flowing.

I noticed that Abby did not take much on her plate, a very little turkey, a small helping of the regular mashed potatoes with a little bit of gravy, and a roll. I didn't say anything, though, because I knew how nauseated I was sometimes, a lot of the time, from chemotherapy treatments, and Abby had just had a massive one with a new drug added. Brett had brought Briana's high chair out and put it up to the table, and she was in her feasting glory. She loved her grandmother's mashed potatoes and was given a heaping helping, one to compete with Mount St. Helen.

Just when I was wondering if I should take second helpings of everything, there was a tap on my shoulder and an urgent sounding whisper in my ear. "Kristen, I need to use your bathroom… right away."

As I rose from the picnic bench seat, I looked around at Mom and Carly and Leigh and Brett. "Would ya'll mind watching Bri? I need to go in with Abby."

They all nodded acceptance and Mom said, "Sure, take your time."

I led the way as fast as I could, knowing that Abby probably needed to be sick. We reached the bathroom door off the kitchen just in time. As she hugged the toilet seat, I put my hand on her back. Somehow, I couldn't see her brother doing this, and didn't know if Abby ever had anyone to comfort her. She lay her head over the seat for about five minutes until she felt better, then flushed the toilet, and backed up to rest sitting against the wall, her arms wrapped around her bent legs. I went to get her a cloth rinsed in ice water from the kitchen.

When I returned and gave her the cloth that she put to her head, I leaned up against the old freestanding claw foot bathtub and looked at the small yellow rose pattern on the wallpaper. I was glad that our bathroom was so large. The yellow rose pattern had always felt soothing to me. Abby looked up and shook her head and gave a little smile. "We have to stop meeting like this," she laughed. I remembered the first day I met Abby at the Infusion Center, when she unexpectedly took off her wig, and we laughed and laughed. Abby was a comrade spirit.

I made my way over to the wall perpendicular to the wall that Abby was resting against and slid down and joined her. We both sat there, on the floor with the bathroom door closed, and just started talking. You would have thought we were at a scheduled tea.

"Kris, yesterday, when you were talking about remembering Bible stories you learned as a child, I envied you. We didn't go to church, and I don't know any Bible stories."

I was aghast but tried not to show it. I couldn't imagine someone not knowing *any* Bible stories from childhood. What about the one where Jesus says to let the little children come? What about David and Goliath? I couldn't imagine going through what we were both going through without any faith.

"Maybe I can teach you some," I said.

Abby continued, "Your faith, when you told me that you had decided to give Billy Ray and the rape to God, at least for the time being, you seemed to have an answer where there was no answer. You believed in a God you could not see and a way you didn't know." She looked puzzled. "You seemed to trust him with your heart."

I looked at her and shook my head. "Trust me, Abby, I have to be reminded all the time. Remember... this rape happened almost three years ago. I didn't trust God then. I just ran."

"Do you think God wants him punished?" she asked.

"I don't know about punished, but I don't think it's loving to me or him or the community at large to let it go. Billy Ray committed a sin against me, and I let his sin take me away, isolate me, and drag me into darkness. I let his sin have a foothold in my life. I don't think you can resolve anything without confronting it."

She looked at me like she was deeply pondering what I had said, like it made a material difference to her life.

"And Billy Ray... is it loving to let him persist in sin?" I asked. "If God loves Billy Ray as much as He loves you and me, the thought made me shiver, I don't think he wants him allowed to run fancy free and continue in the same direction. Not to mention, I wonder if he has raped any other women since me, or heaven forbid a child. I have guilt feelings about that."

Abby reached over and put her hand on my knee. "Kristen, I think if you were able to deal with it then, you would have. It sounds like it threw you for a loop."

What an incredible friend I had made.

"Want a banana popsicle?" I asked. I thought it may settle her stomach.

"Do you have root beer?"

"I just might."

Just then, there was a knock on the bathroom door. It was Johnny. "Hey, you two OK in there?"

We both looked at each other and laughed. Then, we rose to our feet and opened the door. Johnny rushed in to take his turn.

I got out a banana popsicle from the frig for me and a root beer one for Abby, and we sat down at the kitchen table. I propped my right leg up with my foot on the chair and relished the iced banana flavor. What an unusual Thanksgiving, I thought. Abby was looking much better and, at that moment, I felt within me that it was divine providence that we were supposed to meet. I knew that God loved her as much as he loved me. I didn't know His purpose, but I knew there was a purpose.

When we had finished our popsicles, Abby asked, "Would you mind if James and I eat and run? I think I want to be home when the next wave of nausea comes over me."

"I totally get it," I said, and I knew that she understood that indeed I did.

I thought that maybe I'd invite her to some of the Christmas activities at our little church, but that would be later when she was feeling better. "I'm so glad you came. I'll call you next week."

"Thanks," she said as she got up to leave and go get James.

I followed her out and thanked James for coming. "Maybe we'll see each other again," I said.

The rest of the guests stayed until the dinner was done and the tables cleared. Leigh and Carly stayed and helped Mom put leftovers away and do dishes. I was beginning to get tired and got relieved from any kitchen duty. As I collapsed onto the front porch glider to watch Briana play with Lucky, Brett came over. He bent down and gently gave me a kiss on the side of my neck. "I need to stop by my parents today," he said. I knew he could see I was tired so didn't ask me to go.

I looked at him and smiled. "Thanks for coming, and thanks for taking Briana on an outing this morning." I watched him as he walked down the front porch steps with that quick gait of his and leave to visit his parents.

The Friday after Thanksgiving is a big day in Apalachicola as Santa arrives on a shrimp boat at the City Dock to usher in the Christmas season. I coaxed Briana into going to bed early that Thanksgiving night. Actually, I was very tired out from such a full day with so many guests at the house, and I went to bed with her.

Mom gave her a bath for me, and then we picked out some story books and settled in the bedroom rocking chair. She lay in the crook of my left arm, all clean and snuggly in her soft pajamas as we read one story book after another. I loved reading Briana stories, it was a ritual I had started early in her life, and I wanted to suspend time. We read until her little eyelids were so heavy that I knew she'd be asleep as soon as I put her down.

* * * * *

The next day, we all lazied around until it was time to go to Apalachicola and see Santa arrive on a shrimp boat. Mom, Leigh, Carly and I were as excited as any child on Christmas morning. Although Jacob teased and made fun of us, he was sure not to miss it. He could after all use little Briana as an excuse to be there even though he was in middle school. Brett had planned to meet us there at the City Dock.

As we drove into Apalachicola just before twilight, the streets were lined with luminaries and historic homes were decorated and aglow with Christmas lights. Carolers' voices filled the air as they walked the streets of downtown.

A small crowd was beginning to gather at the waterfront dock, with children and adults alike anticipating the arrival of Santa. Even in late November, there were seagulls flying overhead in anticipation of children tossing up goodies for them to catch. As the sun was setting, you could see the outline of a shrimp boat in the distance, slowly making its way to shore. A flock of sea gulls escorted it in. You could hear the voices of children as the majestic boat approached. "I can see it," and "He's coming," could be heard.

When Buddy's Boy shrimp boat got closer, you could see Santa standing at the helm with his bag full of goodies. The metal outriggers that are spread out when the boat is trawling were in upright position. It looked like God was bringing in his blessings on angel wings. How can a mall Santa ever compete with that? As the shrimp boat glided to the dock, the crowd cheered.

"Ho, Ho, Ho!" Santa said as he stepped off the boat when it docked. He made his way through the crowd of eager children and adults to the stand that was set up with his Adirondack chair for him to hear Christmas wishes. All the children scurried over to get in line.

Brett had been holding Briana when the boat glided in and Santa arrived. She just looked on in amazement, more enthralled with what everyone was so excited about. We waited in line for her to see Santa and get her picture taken. The closer we got to the front of the line, the more apprehensive she seemed to get. I wished the Santa in the chair could give me what I wanted for Christmas. I wished he could assure that my little girl would have her mother while she went through all the growing up stages. I wished he could cure my cancer.

When it was finally our turn, Briana did sit on Santa's left knee, but only because her mommy was on his right. Brett snapped a picture, and I wondered, as I had before, who would be the recipient of all the pictures. Who would be able to look back on them and remember this time? I hoped that Briana would.

The weather that evening was beautiful, just cool enough for a heavy sweater or light jacket. We decided to all go over to the Market Street Soda Shop. We walked in and sat on the stools at the counter, Brett holding Bri beside me. Seems like all we did the past two days was eat, and for me that was a feat. The past few days since I was taking a hiatus from cancer treatments that had made an improvement, and had received blood, I had felt like I was among the living. My hair was even beginning to grow back and, in some ways, looked stylish.

As we left the soda shop, we could hear the carolers in the distance. Their sound grew closer and closer until they were caroling along the street in front of us. Briana was so excited and giggled with glee. Mom loves Christmas carols and was singing right along. My heart was just filled with love and happiness that night.

As we drove home back to the Cape, I looked out the window at the expanse of sky and stars. There seemed to be so many stars out as if they were there just for us. I felt contented as I looked over at my daughter, asleep in her car seat.

When we pulled in the drive, Mom invited Leigh and Carly to join us for hot chocolate. Just what we need, I thought, more calories. Mom liked to make it from scratch, and I'm sure it had a thousand. As if we hadn't all had enough to eat and drink the past two days, but, I thought, the holidays only come once a year.

"I'll get the marshmallows," Jacob said.

Fifteen

The Coombs House Inn in Apalachicola is a historic Victorian mansion that was originally built at the turn of the century in 1905 by James N. Coombs, a prominent citizen of the small seaside village. This morning, the Saturday after Thanksgiving, I was to meet Terry, the attorney I had worked for in Tampa, at the Inn for breakfast. Mom had agreed to drop me off on her way to buy groceries at the IGA. I wanted Mom to meet Terry, so we parked in the back of the Inn facing the verandas and both walked up the steps to the back-entrance hall.

Terry had alerted the innkeeper to expect us. The woman who greeted us at the door as we entered made me feel like I had known her forever and was coming home on break from college, or that my mom and I were family coming back home for the holidays. She escorted us into the dining room off the main entrance hall where Terry was sitting at a small two-person table against an interior wall.

As we approached her table, Terry rose from her chair and extended her hand to Mom. "Hi, I'm Terry Matheson."

"This is my mother, Jenna Parker," I said as I motioned toward my mom.

"Nice to meet you. We have so missed your daughter at the firm."

"I know she's missed you all, too. I am so glad, though, that she's home," my mom said as she looked my way and gave me a soft gentle smile.

"I wanted Mom to come in and meet you, but now she's going to be doing some shopping in town and then can pick me up about ten. Do you think that time would be OK?"

"That time would be fine." Then, she looked at my mom and asked, "Are you sure you wouldn't like to have some breakfast. I'm really impressed with this inn. They're serving baked strata this morning, and they have warm muffins and fresh fruit." She motioned over to the antique side table.

"I'd love to, but I'm sure you and Kristen have a lot to talk about."

I waved goodbye to Mom as I joined Terry at the table.

Terry was in her upper forties, although I always thought of her as younger. She was vibrant and energetic and always came up with just the right strategy for any case we were working on. This morning, as at work, she wore her mid-length ash hair pulled back in a barrette, and, even with her designer jeans, she wore a blazer. I wondered if Terry ever let her hair down, both literally and figuratively speaking. I wondered if she ever lounged around even half a day in her robe and slippers, or better yet, her pajamas or an old oversized T-shirt.

"Kristen," she said as she slid a sealed yellow greeting card envelope across the table. "This is from everyone. We have all been wondering how you are."

I opened the envelope to find a get-well card signed by what looked like everyone in the firm. There was also a check for $540.

"We didn't know what you could use, so we all chipped in," Terry said.

"Terry, this is way beyond," I responded as I looked up at her. "Let everyone know I very much appreciate it. It's hard when you don't have any income coming in."

Just then, another woman with an apron on came out of the kitchen and walked over to our table. She described the baked fare of the day that she would serve from the kitchen and also invited me to help myself to the warm muffins, fresh fruit, yogurts, juice, coffee and tea that were on the side table.

As she motioned to the antique side table up against another interior wall, I glanced around the room. It was a very elegant dining room with a large antique table and chairs in the center, probably to seat large families or friends who had gathered together, or for guests to get to know one another. There was a very large interestingly artistic dried floral arrangement in the center of the main table. Other small tables for two or three were scattered along the sides. At the back of the dining room was a beautiful sitting area with antique furniture up against a backdrop of long vertical windows. There were old fashioned built-ins on one side of the room with books of an earlier era.

I graciously ordered the baked strata with sausage and went to make myself a cup of tea at the side table. I'd had coffee earlier at home and now opted for a change. When I returned, I knew it was time for the serious talk that she had come all this way for.

"Terry, when I first arrived at the Cancer Center, they gave me steroids for pain. Remember how much my back hurt before I left Tampa?"

Terry nodded.

"Then, I had radiation treatments to shrink the cancer before receiving chemotherapy treatments. I've had three cycles of chemotherapy now, and my cancer is still not completely gone. The doctors say that the small-cell cancer I have is terminal. It had already spread, metastasized, before I even knew I had it." I paused and then proclaimed, "I am still fighting it though with everything I have."

Terry reached her hand across the table and put it on mine. "I am so sorry to hear that," she said.

The woman came from the kitchen and brought my baked hot strata with sausage. "I hope you like it," she said.

This interruption gave Terry a chance to excuse herself briefly to pour another cup of coffee from the side table. "I will just be a minute," she said as she picked up her coffee mug and rose to excuse herself.

So there I sat, teacup in hand, in a collision of worlds. Cape San Blas and this small quaint seaside village of Apalachicola were in my body and soul. The beauty and simple way of life entered the pores of my being from every direction. How many times had I sat looking out the closed window on a rainy Saturday in Tampa and yearned to feel the soft breeze on the Cape or smell the fresh sea air? Yet, since I'd returned, never had I yearned for the corporate busy world of Tampa. I knew what I had to do.

When Terry returned to our small table, I placed my teacup down on its saucer and looked directly into her eyes. "Terry, I'm not going to get better, not all the way. And even if I do, I won't be returning to Tampa."

"We were afraid of that," she said, "but you never know, you may beat this thing."

It was clear to me that Terry didn't understand the gravity of what I had just said. It wasn't just the terminal cancer. I felt in sync here, my body, mind, and spirit. This is where I belonged.

"Kristen, the firm decided before my trip that if this was the case, we could keep you on the books for another three months, so you have time to make other arrangements for health insurance. I know that COBRA is offered, but I think it's probably about six or seven hundred dollars a month. You can call Sue in Human Resources, and she can give you all the information."

"Thank you for giving me three more months," I heard my mouth saying. Inside, I thought, what's three months? I had loved working for Terry and hoped to be like her one day, but in three months our relationship would be over because of a change in circumstances. Oh, I knew she would send me cards, and, heaven forbid if I die, flowers, but our work relationship had been the extent of our connection. I knew I would probably never see her on this earth again.

I was sitting facing the dining room entrance and noticed a young man *who looked like Brett* standing just beyond it in the foyer talking with the innkeeper. He was facing the fireplace on the opposite wall, so I only saw him from behind. He had a tablet and pen and was engaged in conversation.

"Terry, I think I see someone I know. Let me check," I said as I got up and walked out to see if it was indeed Brett. As I came around his left side, I turned and looked. It *was* Brett.

"Hi Kris," he said as soon as he saw me.

"You know each other?" the innkeeper chortled.

"Yes, this is my good friend Kristen Parker."

"Nice to meet you," I said as I extended my hand.

Then, I turned back to Brett, "I'm having breakfast with Terry, the attorney I used to work for in Tampa. She's staying here. What are you doing here?"

"Oh, I visit the Inn often," he said, "whenever they are doing new constructing or renovating." I should have known as Brett was now the building inspector.

"Kris, have you ever been here before?" he asked as he pointed over to the carved oak staircase? "The renovations have been quite impressive."

"It's beautiful," I said. I looked at the innkeeper and then to Brett. "When you're free, I'd like you to meet Terry. We're seated at a small table on the side."

The innkeeper motioned for Brett to go ahead and then meet him after.

I introduced Brett to my former employer and then Mom arrived. I was very glad to see her. As much as I genuinely liked Terry, I didn't know what else I could say to her. Oh, I could ask about the Bassett case or if she had found research for the Saunders litigation, but did it really matter to me now? No, it didn't.

Brett was polite and excused himself to go back to work. I gave Terry a hug and told her how much I had enjoyed working for her and wished the firm well. Mom extended her hand and said, "Nice meeting you."

I left the Inn that morning with such clarity. It was as if that chapter in my life had just been closed with breakfast and a handshake. Now, I could get on with the business of truly living... for however long that would be.

Mom and I hadn't been in the car three minutes when her cell phone rang. Mom had a cell phone for work in Franklin County Schools which included Apalachicola, Carrabelle, and Eastpoint, but it wouldn't work when she was out on the Cape.

"Hello," she answered. "Sure, Carly, she's right here," Mom said as she passed the phone to me.

"Kris, I was just in town picking up some fish for dinner at the fish market on Waters when I saw your dad with Viola Peters again. She was strutting around like a peacock."

I gasped and looked over at Mom.

Carly continued, "The Riverfront Inn seems to be where they meet. I checked with Leigh, and she was picking up some things for her cats at that delightful store in town for pets, I think it's called Petunia's. Anyway, it's just around the corner, and she said she'd pay and head right over to scope them out. I'm on standby close by, parked in front of Boss Oyster."

"Hold on," I said as I lowered the receiver and filled Mom in on what Carly had said.

Mom pulled over and put her hands up to her face, covering her nose and mouth in prayer fashion, and sighed heavily into them like, *What do I do now?* When she had finished with her shocked reaction, she resolutely put her hands back on the wheel and turned the car around heading back in to town.

"Carly, we're on our way," I said into the phone.

"Ten four."

We pulled up in the Boss Oyster restaurant parking lot next to Carly and waited with our windows down. Leigh would call us when she knew something and could. In about ten minutes, Carly's cell phone rang.

Mom and I waited anxiously to hear what Leigh had uncovered. This wasn't the first sleuth undertaking we'd embarked upon as the *Fabulous Four*. We sat patiently and waited to be briefed.

When Carly clicked off her phone and turned to us, we were ready for the facts. What had Leigh seen? What had she uncovered, if anything?

"Leigh followed them, and they're in Room 106," Carly said. "She's standing by out of sight in case they leave."

I looked at Mom. "What do you want to do?"

"Wait here. I'm going to knock on the door and confront them."

As soon as Mom was out of sight, Carly and I crept out of our cars to follow her. I wasn't sure what Miss *Peacock* would do, and I wanted to protect Mom.

We went across to the Riverfront Inn parking lot and through the walkway between the office and lodge rooms. With our backs up against the left wall, I peered around the corner – Mom was in front of us on her way to the room. We waited.

I heard a loud knock. No answer. Then, another loud knock. No answer. It was quiet for about five minutes. I peered around the corner again, and Mom was leaning up against the wooden railing as the rooms faced the river. It was apparent that Mom was not going anywhere until one of them opened the door.

All of a sudden, you could hear a slow scrunching sound. The door was opening. Carly and I made our way around to see. Dad and Miss *Peacock* were just standing there together looking out.

"I want to talk with my husband," Mom said as she looked at Viola Peters.

"He ain't your husband," Miss *Peacock* replied.

"What a stupid thing to say!" Mom said with a raised voice.

In places like Apalachicola, everyone knew everyone, and everyone knew Mom and Dad were married. Everyone also knew Viola Peters had been married three times before. Her last two husbands had died under mysterious circumstances, and Viola Peters had collected on large life insurance policies. Dad knew that. What was he thinking?

Mom stood there and looked at Dad... and he didn't move. He just stood there.

Then, Mom left in a hurried huff, shaking her head from left to right with her lips pressed together.

Leigh and I were dumbstruck and followed Mom as fast as we could as she apparently couldn't get away fast enough. We were almost running to keep up with her. When we got to the cars, Mom got in the driver's seat and just wanted to go home.

"We've got groceries that need to go in the freezer," Mom said. "Let's get home."

Carly looked at me and I looked at her, and we waved goodbye and went our separate ways.

Sixteen

Life is an unfolding mystery. We never know what the next day will bring. It was about three a.m. and the stillness and darkness of the early morning was all around me when I called out, "Help! Help! Mom! Mom!" There was no answer. She didn't hear me, and Dad wasn't home in the house. He may have been down in his workshop, or he may have been at Viola Peters', but he wasn't here when I needed him.

I couldn't breathe! I called out again as best I could to Mom. Lucky didn't even hear me. Without my breath, I couldn't get up. I rolled off the bed and crawled as best I could toward my mom and dad's room. Then, she heard me.

"Kristen!" she exclaimed as she came out of her room and saw me on the floor.

"I can't breathe!" I managed to say.

Just then Jacob came out of his room and Mom called over to him, "Jacob, call 911. We need paramedics. Your sister can't breathe."

I know both Jacob and my mom were worried. Sometimes, it took longer than normal for paramedics to get out on the Cape. The good thing was that they had been out before and knew directions to our house. Mom did the best she could to keep me calm, comfortable, and breathing until they arrived.

We were never so glad to see someone in our whole lives. Little Briana slept through it all, thank the Lord. As soon as the paramedics arrived, one immediately put an oxygen mask over my face. The other took his stethoscope and listened to my chest. Mom filled them in on my history of small cell cancer that originated in my lungs. Immediately, it was surmised that one of my lungs had collapsed. That was what was making it hard for me to breathe. As soon as they got me stabilized, they put me on a stretcher and transported me to the nearest hospital which happened to be in Port St. Joe. Mom followed in her car, and Jacob stayed at home to watch Briana.

We hadn't planned on spending five hours in the emergency room that morning. When am I ever going to learn that I'm not in control? The best laid plans...

The doctor walked over with my open chart, pen in hand, to address my mother and me. "Miss Parker, we're going to admit you. As soon as possible, you need to have your lungs aspirated."

Aspirated? What's that? I wondered with a fearful expression on my face.

The doctor continued, "A needle will be inserted through your back to draw liquid out that has been accumulating in your lungs. You should feel much better when it's over."

When it's over? I thought. What about when it's happening?

I could tell that Mom was in pain for me.

They didn't know what time I would have my lungs aspirated. After I was admitted and settled in a room, Mom went home to be with Briana, so Jacob could go to school. It was a juggling act. Where was Dad? I wondered. He could help with Briana or be with me. How hard could it be to know I needed him?

I had given the nurse in the emergency room my list of medications, fifteen in all. When they wheeled me down to have my lungs aspirated, they made sure I had been given anti-anxiety medication. Everyone said I was so brave during the procedure – did I have a choice? I wondered. That moving path I had been thrust onto when I became a member of this selective club had many tasks

I needed to complete that weren't options. If I wanted to live, I had no choice.

As soon as the task of the day, a procedure to aspirate my lungs, was completed, Mom was allowed to take me home. I was so tired and just wanted to sleep. When we walked in the kitchen door, I realized that Dad was there. Little did I know that a major conversation was slated to take place that would make a material difference in my life.

My mom started the conversation, "Kristen, we need to talk about something we've been putting off that I think may be helpful now."

"I need to lie down," I said as I made my way through the kitchen and into the living room to lie on the sofa. Mom gently lifted my feet as she slipped under them to sit on the sofa with me. Dad sat in an adjacent chair.

"Kristen, we are fighting this cancer, and I hope and pray we win. I know that when hospice was mentioned by Dr. Kerns, we didn't think we needed it. You still had your health insurance through work, and we had been able to manage the co-pays for your prescriptions. Now, your prescriptions are astronomical, and you will be losing your insurance soon."

"Mom, I don't want to give up."

"Kristen, we aren't giving up. Hospice does not have the same guidelines for service that they used to have. They used to be only for those people who had been given six months or less to live… and you couldn't have hospice and still receive treatment. That's no longer the case. We can have hospice and still fight and win. If we have hospice, Kris, they will provide all your medications."

"Does it have to change my life? Can I still stay home?"

"It doesn't have to change anything, except make it easier for us. They will come to our house to provide services, as many or as few as we need or want."

Dad had been quietly sitting in the chair, his hand cupping his chin, his fingers going back and forth on his light whiskers. He leaned forward to me as if he had been giving it a great deal of thought while Mom had been talking.

"It seems to me… the bottom line is that the many medications that you need are very expensive. If we accept hospice services, they will provide all your medications for free. Kristen, we aren't giving up, just trying to get as much help for you as we can."

"And," Mom jumped in, "we can still continue with Dr. Kerns and all the treatments he and the Cancer Center have. You will have a hospice nurse who will come out and monitor your progress and be here when we need her and coordinate with Dr. Kerns at the Center."

I didn't want to admit that I was eligible for hospice, that I may be dying, but it would be nice not to have to worry if I could afford my medications. My pain would not be bearable without the heavy doses of narcotics they had me on. It would be impossible without them.

"Kristen, we could try hospice services, and, if you don't like them, cancel them at any time."

"OK, Mom, let's try …but I can cancel them at any time, right?"

"Right. I'll give them a call and make an appointment for them to come out and begin services."

As Mom dialed the number, I wondered how invasive or intruding into my life the services would be. I didn't want a Nurse Rachet telling me what to do.

I was asleep on the sofa when I heard a faint knock on the front door. My mom came from the kitchen to answer it. A woman with a doctor's bag and a nice-looking middle-aged man entered.

Once she was in the front door, the woman extended her hand to Mom. "Hi, I'm Alice Weaver, the hospice nurse, and this" she said, as she motioned to the man with her, "is Michael Carson, the hospice social worker."

I opened my eyes and blinked sleepily as I stretched and slowly sat up on the end of the sofa.

"This is my daughter, Kristen Parker," my mom said.

Alice was first, "Nice to meet you, Kristen."

Then Michael, "Hi, Kristen."

Alice and Michael explained the same things Mom and Dad had... that hospice would provide all my medications and monitor me and communicate with Dr. Kerns. Alice would be my assigned nurse and visit me once a week. A nurse would be on call 24/7 for us to call if something unexpected came up and we needed them. Michael was a hospice social worker who would be there for all of us but specialized in children. He would be there if we needed him to counsel Jacob and Briana just by getting to know them and through play therapy.

It seemed like Alice and Michael were there forever that day. Alice took my blood pressure, listened to my heart and asked me a myriad of questions. It must have taken twenty minutes just for her to copy down all of my medications. Michael was just genuinely friendly and supportive. When Jacob came home from school, he introduced himself, and they played a game of cards while Alice was finishing up all her questions.

It was a very long day. Mom made homemade chicken and dumplings for dinner. It was only Mom, Jacob, Briana and me. Ever since my dad had been caught with Viola Peters, he wasn't living at home. Mom must have asked him to come today for the "hospice" decision. As delicious as dinner was, I couldn't make it through. I was so very tired and left the table to go to bed.

"Mom, will you take care of Bri tonight?"

"Of course, Kris."

"Thanks," and then I went to bed and was out like a light.

The next morning, I awoke with Briana at my bedside. She had climbed out of her little bed and had come over to watch Mommy sleep. I opened my eyes to see her staring right back at me.

"Good morning, Bri. Want to snuggle?"

A big smile crossed her face and she hopped right up into bed with me as I put my hands underneath her arms and helped her up.

Today, I would spend the day with her. We would read stories and snuggle and go for a walk along the shore, picking up seashells. We would eat popsicles and maybe make cutout Christmas cookies with frosting and red and green sugar sprinkles. Today, I would make the most of my time with my little girl. I may not know how many days I have left on this earth, but I have today.

"Good morning, girls," Mom said as she peeked into my bedroom and saw we were both up and snuggling in my bed. She was already dressed for work. "Is Briana going to preschool today?"

"Actually, I'm feeling pretty good at the moment, and I think Briana and I are going to take the day off and just spend it together."

"Well, if you don't feel well later in the day, please call me, and I'll make sure this little one gets to her school."

"Will do. Thanks, Mom."

And Mom was out the door.

As I heard the kitchen door latch and Mom's car back out of the driveway, I felt like it was a vacation day just beginning. Mom was at work and Jacob was at school. Briana and I stayed in our pajamas until almost noon. We had breakfast and read story after story after story. Then, we got dressed and walked across to the beach side of the Cape closest to our house. I didn't want to risk walking down the peninsula and across the dunes to my favorite place on the beach, my favorite place on earth, not after what had happened with my lungs yesterday. We picked up so many seashells, Briana examining each one. When we got back to my parent's bungalow, we both collapsed in our beds and took a little nap.

I had forgotten that to make Christmas cutout cookies, the batter would need to be made ahead and chilled in the refrigerator. I would ask Mom to help me with it tonight. Instead, I got out the art paper and finger paints, and Briana and I set about making pictures, pictures of the beach, of our bungalow, of Brett, and of Lucky.

When our pictures were dry, I told my beautiful little daughter that she could put her picture on the refrigerator with one of the magnets. She gently took her work of art, opened the refrigerator door, and carefully placed it on the middle shelf. My heart melted. Then, she took a bottled water that was on the kitchen table from when I had been drinking it during our finger painting and said, "Lucky wants a drink."

"OK, I said, you can give Lucky a drink."

She took the bottle and poured it in Lucky's water dish, then went to the silverware drawer to get him a straw. I had to laugh when Lucky went over and actually put his mouth on the straw.

My dearest Briana, I thought. If only I had a camera, I could take a picture of all the cute things you do, but when could I look back at them and remember? Could I take the pictures with me to have in heaven? I don't think so… but I'll have you in my heart.

I pulled out my journal from the end table drawer as I sat up against one of the sofa pillows in the corner, my legs drawn up to the side. I began a new entry where I had left off and talked to my dearest little girl Briana. I was so scared after what had happened the day before, my lung collapsing. I feared that no one could take care of my little girl the way that I could, that no one knew her favorite book and the things she loved. I expressed my feelings to my little daughter that one day she might read. As I closed the journal and put it away, tears began to stream down my face. They were bittersweet tears – tears of sadness that I may not be on this earth as long as my little daughter needs me, tears of joy for the blessing that God had given me of my little girl and of this day, this one special day.

That night after dinner, Briana and I went out on the front porch and picked out the moon. Where was God, I wondered, when my world seemed to be falling apart. Was He still in control?

Seventeen

It's weird... never knowing what each new day will bring, but then, do we ever?

"Kristen, telephone," my mother called from the kitchen.

I wondered who it could be. I had just talked with Brett earlier on the phone. It was Saturday, and he wanted to know if we could make plans to do something later in the day. He would be over... and could he bring me a latte? Carly was visiting her sister and brother-in-law in Orlando. They had just had a baby, making her officially an aunt for the first time. And Johnny... Johnny would just come over. He wouldn't call. My world seemed to have grown smaller since I'd been back home, just close friends and family.

"Hi Kristen, it's Abby."

I could hear her smile across the phone lines. Abby was just one of those spirits who always had a smile, and, whenever she smiled, her eyes sparkled.

"Sounds like you're feeling better," I said.

"Much. Thanks again for having us over for Thanksgiving."

"Abby, I was so glad you could come, and everyone enjoyed meeting you and your bother."

"Kristen, I was just in town and saw this notice on the counter up front at the pizzeria when I was paying. It was advertising a special guest singer for a Christmas service tomorrow at Pioneer Methodist Church. Isn't that the church you told me you grew up in?"

"Yes, and my family still goes there. I have been going whenever I'm not sick or have the energy."

"Do you think I could go with you tomorrow… if you're feeling up to it?"

"Sure, Briana likes going. They have a Sunday School for her while we're in church."

"Great, should I just meet you there?"

"You know where it is?" I asked.

"Yes, I've passed by it many times."

"OK, why don't I call you as soon as we're ready to leave the house? Brett is meeting us there, too."

"Sounds good. I'll be waiting for your call."

Unbelievable, I thought, as I hung up the phone. This would be the first time Abby *ever* went to church… and here she was calling me to see if she could come.

Mom was busy making tuna fish sandwiches… and peanut butter and jelly for Bri.

"Mom, are they having a special singer at church tomorrow?" I asked.

"Yes, Thelma Sue's brother-in-law is visiting, and I think he has some famous artist with him. Reverend Dave said that one of his songs is perfect for the sermon he's preaching – *For Such a Time as This*. I think it's about how Jesus was born for a purpose… for such a time as this. Anyway, it should be pretty good."

"Well, Abby saw a flyer in town about it and asked to come. Can you believe it? She's going to meet us there. Remind me to call her just before we leave."

"Will do."

The next morning seemed to come awful early. I had taken a shower the night before, so I could conserve my energy and maybe make it through the church service. Mom reminded me to call Abby.

"Hi Abby. It's Kris. Still want to go to church this morning?"

"Yes, I'm all ready. I was just waiting on your call."

"We're leaving now, so I'll see you there. Let's meet at the front double doors going into the church. That's where Brett will meet us."

"Great, see you there."

When we arrived, Dad was there in the camper waiting for us. He walked up, and Briana went running to him. "Pop Pop!"

"How's my Queen Bee?" Dad asked as he scooped her up. Then he turned to me. "Do you want me to take her to her Sunday School?"

I looked around and didn't see Miss Peacock, but I wasn't going to touch that subject with a ten-foot pole, not today at least. "Sure," I said. I reached over and gave Briana a kiss. "Have a good time, sweetie."

As we walked up to the front of the church, Abby was waiting. Incredible, I thought. She has never ever been to church, but she seemed anxious this morning. Just then, Brett walked up from the side, his Bible in hand. We all walked in together – Mom, Brett, Abby and me.

Pioneer Methodist is a small country church. I loved looking up at the wooden rafters and the fact that a wooden cross stood firm in the center between the two pulpits. A lot of churches in Tampa were non-denominational and didn't have a cross anywhere to be seen in the sanctuary. We still had the wooden boards with slats in the front, the one on the right showed how many people had been in Sunday school and church that day and how much offering had been taken in, and the one on the left had the hymnal pages displayed. We sat in the pew together – Mom, Abby, me, and then Brett. I noticed Mom left a space for Dad on the end. I wasn't quite sure what that was about.

Most of the service was predictable – We always sang *Trust and Obey* and *What a Friend We Have in Jesus*. It occurred to me, though, that maybe Abby had never heard these songs. When Hannah Evans got up to read the scripture before the sermon, she told the Christmas story from Luke. I imagined how this reading would sound if you were hearing it for the first time. Abby just sat beside me in the pew, quiet and wide-eyed. Then, Reverend Dave got up to deliver his sermon – *For Such a Time as This.*

At first, Reverend Dave was quiet. He looked out over all his parishioners, his open Bible in his hand, as if he was pondering what to say. Then, he began.

"Such a simple story, and yet…"

He paused. You could have heard a pin drop.

"…the love story behind it is beyond extraordinary and far-reaching."

After some time of silence, he continued again, "Just the mere fact that God chose to live with mankind and teach us all that he did in his short life, just thirty-three years, shows how very much we matter to him. We counted on God when he gave us such a far-reaching gift, and we still do."

Reverend Dave asked the congregation to turn over to John 8:19. Brett took his Bible that he had set down on the pew beside him and turned the pages until he reached the passage. Then, he put it between us, his left arm resting on the top of the pew behind my shoulders.

"'*You do not know me or my Father,' Jesus replied. 'If you knew me, you would know my Father also.*'" God wanted us to know him and sent his son to walk among us. He wanted relationship with us. As the song we're going to hear a little later says "*Right now, I really have no choice …But to voice the truth to the nations …A generation looking for God.*" Jesus had a purpose. He was born for a specified time, for a special purpose, *for such a time as this.*"

Reverend Dave went back to John 8, verse 20:
He spoke these words while teaching in the temple area near the place where the offerings were put. Yet no one seized him, because his time had not yet come.

"The scripture made note of those who wanted to harm Jesus," said Reverend Dave, "yet no one did because his time had not yet come. God was in control. Jesus, just like you and me, was born for a purpose, and we will live the time needed to fulfill that purpose."

He looked over to a man sitting in the front row and said, "We are very fortunate today to have Wayne Watson, who is visiting here with one of our families this week, to sing for us." At that introduction, the man got up and went to the front and took a microphone he had waiting and began to sing. It was as if the words were written for me, especially the first verse –

Now, all I have is now
To be faithful, To be holy, And to shine Lighting up the darkness.
Right now, I really have no choice
But to voice the truth to the nations A generation looking for God.

As he began to sing the chorus, I couldn't help but think of Abby, sitting right beside me, and how I had met her, and if my purpose didn't have something to do with her.

For such a time as this
I was placed upon the earth
To hear the voice of God
And do his will
Whatever it is.
For such a time as this
For now and all the days he gives
I am here, I am here, And I am His
For such a time as this.

When the second verse started, I couldn't believe it. It was as if God was directly talking to me –

You – do you ever wonder why
Seems like the grass is always greener
Under everybody else's sky
But right here, right here for this time and place
You can live a mirror of his mercy
A forgiven image of grace.

Had I thought the grass was greener when I ran away to Tampa? Did I think I could run away from my problems? And right here, in this time and place… did God have a purpose for me? Am I that important to Him? As he sang the chorus again, I just couldn't believe that this was the one song that he was singing on this particular day in my church. When he went into the bridge to sing the chorus the climactic last time, it was as if this song had indeed been written for me.

Can't change what's happened till now
But we can change what will be
By living in holiness
That the world will see Jesus.

Then, there was a building crescendo and solo to symphony with the chorus again. I thought my breath would be taken away. I looked over at Abby and just took her hand. Maybe that was all I could do. Our guest singer finished his song, and you could hear a lot of amens in the congregation.

When we all walked out of church that day, I felt blown away. We picked up Briana from her Sunday School classroom, and Brett invited us all out to dinner. Life seemed so full.

That night, as the sun was beginning to set, I walked over to the sea side of the Cape closest to home and just sat there. I noticed a wave of light going across the water. It was the lighthouse. The words to the song reverberated in my ear -

And to shine Lighting up the darkness

The thought of Abby came back to me. Again, I wondered if I had met her for a reason. I remembered that first day I met her at the Infusion Center and wondered why God would make me wait for an appointment with Dr. Kerns when I was in pain. I wondered if Abby was somehow part of my destiny. *All things work together for good*, my mom had said.

Eighteen

The Christmas season passed with the annual pre-Christmas tea of the Fabulous Four and a Christmas Day with an avalanche of presents under the tree. I didn't see much of Dad, but he was there on Christmas Day. I think he knew not to bring Miss Peacock, as we referred to her, around Mom. Rather than confront the issue so they could get past it, Dad escaped... escaped to his boat building project, to the waters of the St. Vincent Sound, and to Viola Peters.

As time passed, my life went in cycles, as did my chemotherapy. My cancer would progress, and we'd try another round of chemotherapy drugs. It would make me sick... and I'd lose my hair... again. When the pain intensified and became almost unbearable, Carly would keep me in wine... in addition to all the many narcotics I was on. For a time, while I was getting chemotherapy treatments, I would sometimes be confined to my bed and look as though death was imminent within days.

Then, the chemo would apparently have worked, although not enough to totally knock out my cancer, and I would be granted a reprieve. I would have a life again and be able to enjoy my time with my family and friends. Brett and I became a couple again. When he wasn't at work, he was at my home on the Cape. He and my little daughter got along famously. When I wasn't feeling well and had no energy at all, he would stop by and pick her up and take her to get ice cream at the Market Street Soda Shop in Apalachicola or to the movies in Panama City. He became an integral part of her life.

I was thankful for the periods of reprieve, and most days went smoothly. One day, though, Carly and I were coming out of the IGA parking lot, waiting on the few cars to pass before we entered the road to turn left. Even the main roads in Apalachicola, Highway 98 and Market Street, *never* had any traffic. We didn't even have a real traffic light. Oh, we had a blinking light at the main intersection in town where the small shops are, but that wasn't even needed. Carly and I had just bought cheese and crackers to have a small wine and cheese party and were laughing hysterically about something when an old beat up pick-up truck pulled up on the right beside us. How odd, I thought, that it didn't just pull behind us and wait its turn; at least that's what I thought until I looked out the window and *slam*, there was Billy Ray looking right back at me. I thought I would die... right then and there.

His hair was dark and slicked back with grease and he had a smirk on his face, his hands straight ahead on the steering wheel while his head was turned toward me. Then, with a loud screeching sound and a jerk, he took off at what must have been 100 miles per hour... as if that was supposed to impress me... or be a slap in the face. I went pale.

"Kristen, let it go," Carly said.

As much as I tried, I couldn't. The rape had never been resolved and the incident tainted the whole afternoon. Abby joined us later in the day, and the three of us drank the wine and ate the cheese and crackers, commiserating with one another about the fact that Billy Ray was even on the planet. I had let him change my life again. We never did have the get-together we had planned for that evening with some of our other friends.

The day passed and the next day came, and I thought things were back to status quo, at least our new status quo. I had slept most of the morning and was pouring myself a bowl of Cheerios when the kitchen phone rang. I was still in my long white terry robe and barefooted.

"Hello," I answered.

"Hi, is this Kristen Parker?" the man's voice on the other end of the line asked.

"Yes, it is. Who's calling?"

"Kristen, this is Tom Kincaid, the state attorney/prosecutor. Could you come in to my office today?"

"I don't know, Mr. Kincaid. What do you need to see me about?"

"I'd rather talk with you in person when you come in," he said.

"Um," I vocalized as I sucked in my right cheek. "Let me see if I can get a ride in. What time do you want me there?"

"Just as soon as you can come in, I'll be in my office all day."

I hung up the phone and walked back to my bowl and box of Cheerios as I wondered what this could possibly be about. I had just seen Billy Ray yesterday, but what could that possibly have to do with anything?

As I ate breakfast, I thought about who to call for a ride into town. I hated not being able to drive, but I no longer had a car and I wasn't supposed to drive because of all the narcotics I was on. I opted for Johnny, my oldest brother. He had his own business, and maybe he could pick me up and take me into town for awhile.

"Hey, *Son*," I said as soon as I got Johnny on the phone. "Do you think you could swing by here and take me into town for a couple hours? I have some shopping I want to do, just downtown on Market Street."

"Sure, I'm almost done dropping off this load at the packing house. I can pick you up in about twenty minutes."

"Now *Son*, no need to fly. You know you can't get out here on the Cape that fast." Johnny was a fast driver, but a good one. He had been driving since he was seven years old when Mom and Dad got him his first motorcycle, a little 50 cc Honda. He thought the St. Joe Paper

Company fire trails were dirt bike or motorcycle trails that were there just for him. That was after he'd torn up his dirt bike, which was after his little big wheel, which was after his tyke bike. That was just Johnny. "I want you here in one piece," I said.

"I'll see ya," Johnny chuckled. "I'll be there."

"OK *Son*, be careful."

As I hung up the phone, I wondered if Johnny might even pull up before I had time to get dressed, maybe put on a little makeup. I didn't want to divulge the real reason I was going into town. I didn't even know what Mr. Kincaid, Tom as he had asked to be called, wanted to talk with me about.

Johnny pulled up in his work truck, *Parker and Son Seafood and Trucking, Incorporated.* When I heard his tires crunching on the oyster shell drive, I had just barely gotten ready. I told Johnny I wanted to do some shopping at the little shops on Market Street, and he could just let me out in front of the pizzeria. I watched him as he turned the corner to go back to work on the waterfront. Then, I turned and headed down the sidewalk toward the courthouse.

Sue Ella James was at her desk when I walked in. Mr. Kincaid's door was closed. She looked up at me from the papers she was working on, her pen in hand. When she recognized me, she said, "Miss Parker, you can go right in."

Go right in, I thought. What is this about?

I walked over to his door and slowly turned the knob. As I entered the room, my eyes went to the top of a young woman's head that shown over the back of one of the two client chairs facing Mr. Kincaid's desk and away from me. As soon as he saw me, Tom Kincaid motioned me in. I walked up parallel to the empty high-backed client chair on the left and looked over to the one on the right... then, I saw her. "Abby!" I exclaimed. What are you doing here?"

Mr. Kincaid motioned me again. "Have a seat, Miss Parker," he said.

I sat down in the empty chair, continuing to look at Abby.

"Miss Connors," Tom Kincaid explained, "has come to me with a rape case against Billy Ray Sorles."

I looked at Abby.

"Kristen," Abby began as she spoke directly to me. She looked so small and frail in the big chair, her short-cropped hair and eyes like saucers. "Remember when I told you at the Infusion Center that I had dated one of Billy Ray's younger brothers, Buddy Lee?"

I nodded.

"Well, about a year and a half ago, on a Saturday morning, I thought I'd stop by his house and see if he wanted to go to the beach. We had talked about doing something that weekend. I had my two-piece bathing suit on with an open cover-up. Anyway, I walked up the steps of the front porch on their Jim Walter manufactured home and knocked on the door. Billy Ray answered and held the screen door open for me to enter into the living room. I asked if Buddy Lee was home. I hadn't seen his car outside. Billy Ray said that no, he wasn't home, but he motioned me to follow him as if he wanted to show me something. He shut the front door and locked it, and we walked to the back to Buddy Lee's bedroom. I guess I thought that since it was Buddy Lee's bedroom we were heading toward, that it was legitimate. It all happened so fast. Before I knew it, he pushed me down onto the bed and raped me. It was over so fast, she said, slowly shaking her head. I screamed and screamed, but no one heard me. You know, they live out in the middle of the woods on property that backs up to the Apalachicola National Forest. When he climbed off of me, he zipped up his pants and threatened me not to tell a soul."

I just stood there with my mouth hanging open.

"Kristen, you are my friend, and I know all you've been going through. After what you told me yesterday when Carly, you, and I were commiserating over wine and cheese crackers, I decided it was time for me to step up and press charges for *us*. I decided it was time to step up and be your friend."

I know I must have looked confused.

Mr. Kincaid stepped in then, "Miss Connors, Abby, did report the rape immediately when it happened. She called 911 and went to the hospital for an evidence exam. We still have her clothes, the two-piece bathing suit and cover-up, in an evidence box. Then, though, she had second thoughts and asked that we not go through with it."

I couldn't believe what I was hearing.

"Miss Parker," Mr. Kincaid continued, "I'd like to have you testify at the trial based on Williams Rule evidence. That is where similar fact evidence, evidence that is similar to this crime, is allowed to be introduced. You may not have had a case, but what happened to you mimics what happened to my client Miss Connors."

Mr. Kincaid then explained how the charge is sexual battery and is considered a second-degree felony. He also explained the criminal punishment score sheet, that unlawful sexual union against the victim's will, and any threats made during or after the crime, count on that score sheet.

It was a lot to take in. I guess we never know what someone else has gone through… and me meeting Abby on that day back in September… may have been for this reason, for us both to find peace.

Nineteen

Billy Ray was arrested, and his case set for a jury trial. I talked with Mr. Kincaid about my cancer and prognosis, but you can only do so much when scheduling a trial to be timely. It was set for three months away. I guess I should have been thankful that we live in a small county, and there weren't that many serious cases that needed to be set for trial in the first place.

Jury selection proved to be as tedious and difficult as I imagined the trial to be. There would be six jurors and one alternate pulled from a pool of twenty Franklin County citizens who were registered to vote. I wanted to go and be supportive of Abby, at least when I was well enough to, so I planned on attending voir dire, an examination of the preliminary or potential jurors. Brett amazed me when he showed up to take me and sat beside me and Abby through the whole thing. He didn't say a word really, but was just there, strong as a rock.

Neither the prosecution nor the defense could pick their jury, only find ways to have those they thought would not give the verdict they wanted disqualified and eliminated. Part of it, you could say, was luck of the draw to see who was in the jury pool.

The first thing the judge did after declaring the court in session was explain the case to the jurors. This included defining all the terminology – what was sexual battery, what and who were the plaintiff and defendant, who were the witnesses, and what was the jury's job.

Potential jurors were asked if they knew personally or of the plaintiff or defendant or any of the witnesses. They were also asked if there was any reason they knew of that they should be excused from duty, such as any other conflicts of interest or reasons why they couldn't sit through a trial such as illness. Right away, a young woman in the back about twenty-eight raised her hand. When she came forward, it was obvious why she wanted excused. She was as big as a house and probably expecting twins at any moment. Her story to the judge was that her due date was next week, and she had two small children already at home. Her husband had been called for military duty overseas, and she was staying with her mother and father on St. George's Island. I rolled my eyes. I was certain the judge would excuse her, but it would have been nice to have her on the jury, a young, defenseless woman who could look at the size of the defendant.

Another potential juror, a man who looked like he was in his thirties, raised his hand. He told the judge that he had grown up in Franklin County and knew of the defendant. The judge asked him if he knew the defendant personally or had ever had any dealings with him. The young man said that he did not know him personally and had never had any dealings with him, but he knew his reputation. At that, the judge asked if he could be impartial and listen to all the facts and make an unbiased decision as to his guilt in this particular case. The answer was yes, he could.

The last person to raise his hand was a man in his fifties. His story was that he was a supervisor at St. Joe Paper Company and didn't know how they would get along without him. He was a property owner and lived in Franklin County, but he worked at the paper company in Port St. Joe in the adjoining Gulf County.

In the end, the only witness the judge struck for cause was the pregnant young woman whose husband was overseas. It was hard to know who to wish for in the jury. At first glance, I thought women would be more sympathetic to the victim. Then again, you never know. I guess it all depends on their history. Who knew it could be so complicated?

That left a pool of nineteen potential jurors. Mr. Kincaid and the defense attorney had put together a questionnaire to be completed and brought with them to get to know each individual person better and know what questions may need to be explored further. Mr. Kincaid had put such questions as –

Does a woman have the right to say no to sexual advances?
Do you have any sisters?
Are you married?
Do you have any daughters?

The defense attorney had added questions such as –

What should a man reasonably expect from a woman after he has bought her dinner or drinks on a date?

Who should make the financial decisions in a marriage?

Have you ever flirted with or had sexual relations with a member of the opposite sex you had not been dating?

Have you ever been divorced?

The judge would not allow the potential juror to be asked if they had ever been raped. They could, however, ask if they had ever filed or been involved in a lawsuit. That opened up the door to ask further questions that might reveal if they, or someone close to them, had indeed been raped and their attitude and feelings toward the crime.

In the end, we were left with the following six jurors –

Frances Martin, a Caucasian forty-eight-year-old cafeteria worker at the elementary school in Carrabelle. She was a stout woman with her dark mid-length hair pulled back in a barrette. Mrs. Martin was a widow of two years with two grown children, a girl and a boy. Her husband had been a science teacher at the local high school in Carrabelle before his death from a heart attack.

Clarence Johnston, a Caucasian fifty-six-year-old retired military man whose last station was Tyndall Air Force Base. He and his wife had moved to the small seaside village of Apalachicola after his retirement four years ago. The couple had no children.

Betty Sue Conrad, a Caucasian thirty-six-year-old secretary at the Franklin County Courthouse in Apalachicola. She was divorced with two sons.

James Cook, a Black forty-nine-year-old history professor who worked at the community college in Port St. Joe. He was married to a stay-at-home mother of their five children.

Karin Mercedes, a Caucasian forty-two-year-old doctor who had moved to the area recently with her husband. Mr. Mercedes was transferred from Tallahassee to work with the Apalachicola National Estuarine Research Reserve under the Florida Department of Environmental Protection. The couple had one child, an adopted son.

James Michael, a Caucasian forty-eight-year-old operator of a shrimp boat. He and his wife Nora lived in Carrabelle and had no children.

The alternate juror chosen, should something happen to one of the others, was a Caucasian twenty-two-year-old single man who worked at the mini mart on Highway 98. The defense attorney had made sure to eliminate the man in his thirties who knew of Billy Ray's reputation, and the paper company supervisor just lucked out as the six jurors and one alternate were named before it was his turn to be interviewed.

Jury selection took hours. It seemed like this whole drawn out court process did nothing but victimize the victim again, especially if she had cancer and no endurance. This was just the beginning, I thought.

Twenty

After Brett dropped me off at home, I slipped inside the front door, just made it to the living room sofa and collapsed with one leg still hanging over the side. Instantly, I fell asleep and slept for hours. I didn't wake up until I heard Mom coming home from work and in through the kitchen screen door. I stirred and raised my arms sleepily over my head to stretch.

"Mom, is that you?" I called out.

"Yes, Kris," she responded. "I'm putting a pot of coffee on, hazelnut cream. You want a cup?"

"Sure." I knew Mom would not be making coffee for herself this late in the day. Actually, although Mom used to be a coffee drinker, she now enjoyed her *cup of tea*. We had explored every tea cottage or tea room within a hundred-mile radius. Having tea just seemed to be so conducive to the long serious talks we'd been having lately. Mom and I had even been thinking about opening up our own tea cottage in Apalachicola. There wasn't one for miles around. *Kristen and Mom's Tea Cottage*, we would name it. Anyway, Mom was making this coffee for me, and the timing was perfect.

As she entered the room with my steaming hot mug full of coffee, cream and sugar already added, I pushed myself up to a sitting position and snuggled in the corner of the sofa. "Thanks, Mom," I said as I took the mug from her.

She settled in on the other end, and I could see she'd made herself a cup of tea with a sprig of mint. "Well, how'd it go today?" she asked.

"Draining, just draining. It took forever for the jury to be selected... and it was draining just looking at Billy Ray. Actually, I tried not to," I said. "I think, though, that the jury that was finally selected will be a good one. There are actually three men and three women on the jury. One of the women is a school cafeteria worker, one works as a secretary at the courthouse, and one is actually a doctor who just moved here. I don't think she has gotten herself established yet, so I think she has free time. One of the men owns a shrimp boat; I wonder if Dad knows him. He didn't claim knowing any of the witnesses, which I will be, but maybe he didn't make the connection. The alternate is that young guy behind the counter at the mini mart on 98."

Both Carly and Leigh stopped by, so Mom and I transitioned ourselves into the kitchen, and we all sat around the big square table.

"You know what I think we need?" I asked with exclamation.

All eyes looked over at me.

"I think we need a celebration!" I proclaimed.

"Are you nuts?" Carly asked. "With all you're going through, the cancer and the trial, not to mention Abby, so double that, ditto."

I cocked my head to the side and looked up, pondering for a moment.

"I think that's exactly what we need. Remember that verse, Romans 5:3-4 –

> Not only so, but we also rejoice in our sufferings, because we know that suffering produces perseverance; perseverance, character; and character, hope.

I've been thinking a lot about that verse lately."

"Oh, you're a character, all right," Leigh said and laughed.

"You know, maybe she's right," Carly said as she looked around at Mom and Leigh. "If we can't beat 'em, so to speak, let's join 'em. If we can't do anything about having to go through the trials, let's celebrate what we are going to gain from them. I'm not sure what that is," she said looking puzzled, "but I think with the four of us, the *Fabulous Four*... and a little wine, we can figure it out and give God the glory. I'm up for a party," she said as she stood up and waved both her arms above her head.

"The *Fabulous Four* and Abby," I said, emphasizing *and Abby*.

Everyone nodded in agreement.

"Yes, I think Abby has earned an honorary place at this celebration," Mom said.

"Celebration *party*," Carly corrected. "And we need wine, plenty of it. You know the first miracle Jesus performed was to turn water into wine at a wedding celebration."

"Carly, I'll bring wine, too," Leigh offered.

"Where are we having this party?" Mom asked.

Carly cupped her chin with her bent fingers in front and thumb underneath and looked up. "I know just the place," she said. As she brought her head back down, she addressed us with her revelation, "I've been watching my parent's place on the river while they're visiting my sister and her new baby in Orlando for the week. My dad has a pontoon boat that's just the right size and even has a charcoal grill. We can do it up right as we party down the river."

Leigh got a gleam in her eyes. "I'm all for it," she said.

Mom chipped in, "I'll bring the hamburgers and hot dogs, and I think we have some charcoal and lighter around here."

"I'll make some fried green tomatoes," I pitched in. "Jacob has been growing the largest most beautiful tomatoes in the back, and they are just now big and beautifully green. I don't think he'll mind... and I'll make some of that homemade buttermilk ranch dressing to go with it."

"I'll bring the buns and catsup and mustard with the wine," Leigh added.

"...And I'll make sure we have lots of chips," Carly said.

"Settled," I said, "the *Fabulous Four... and Abby* will be having our first celebration to rejoice in our sufferings and trials tomorrow at five o'clock on the river... just before the sunset. We each need to bring a verse and think about what trials we are going through that we can find a purpose in or a silver lining."

"Leave it to Kris," Leigh said.

We all put our hands together in the center of the table, one on top of another. "Tomorrow at five," we all chimed.

"I'll call Abby," I said, "and she can ride with me and Mom."

It was so nice to have something to look forward to rather than treatments at the Infusion Center, the associated nausea, pain that one day was worse than others, and a court hearing. Mom even decided to make homemade potato salad. I should have known... the carbohydrate queen. I called Abby and could hear her smile across the phone lines.

"Yes, I'd love to come," she said after I'd explained the plan. "I'll bring my favorite bread and butter pickles. I still have some I jarred last spring."

"Perfect!" I exclaimed.

"And you can pick me up?"

"Sure can, see you about 4:30."

"Great!"

"Bye."

Abby was eagerly waiting on her front porch steps when Mom and I pulled up, her jar of bread and butter pickles in her hands on her lap. As we arrived at Carly's folks' place on the river, I could see Carly and Leigh down at the boat dock, finishing putting on the Bimini top. When Leigh noticed we had pulled up, she came across the large sparsely wooded side yard to help carry the charcoal and whatever else needed carrying. We loaded everything on board, Carly checked the small motor, and we set off down the river.

Carly was right – the boat was perfect for a celebration party… and as we partied down the river, I felt like Marjorie Rawlings, the Florida pioneer woman who had written *The Yearling* and *Cross Creek*. I had been feeling like an author lately myself when I wrote in my journal, writings to my little daughter. We all put the food out on the table in the center and sat in the cushioned seats around it. Leigh and Mom got the charcoal started in the little grill at the back of the boat. Carly had paper plates, napkins, and plastic silverware in the center of the table, but she had brought her best crystal wine glasses. "Nothing's too good for our celebration," she said. I just sat back and enjoyed the cool breeze as we slowly floated down the river.

When we had finished eating, but were still enjoying our wine, I pulled out my verse and asked everyone if they had brought theirs. To my amazement, they each had a piece of paper. Mine was easy as I'd been thinking about it ever since that day Dad had brought me home from the Infusion Center in the camper, and I fell to the grass sick as a dog. I'll start, I said as I read Romans 5:3-5 –

> *Not only so, but we also rejoice in our sufferings*
> *because we know that suffering produces perseverance;*
> *perseverance, character; and character, hope.*
> *And hope does not disappoint us,*
> *because God has poured out his love into our hearts*
> *by the Holy Spirit, whom He has given us.*

"I'm counting on it," I said. "I mean the hope part. And the purpose or silver lining in my cancer and prognosis is that it brought me back home to the Cape. I have smiled more, danced more, and found more joy since I have been home this past year than I may have found in a lifetime if God had not allowed it to happen. Maybe the depth of our joy is only as deep as our sorrow. And," I said as I looked at Abby, "I found a new friend because of it."

"Don't forget Brett," Carly chipped in. "I know he's the love of your life, and he loves you even without hair. If you hadn't been diagnosed with cancer and lost your hair, you'd never know."

"You've got a point," I said.

"OK, Carly, what verse did you bring and what tragedy or trial are you celebrating?"

"James 1:2-4," she said.

> *Consider it pure joy, my brothers,*
> *whenever you face trials of many kinds,*
> *because you know that the testing of your*
> *faith develops perseverance.*
> *Perseverance must finish its work so that*
> *you may be mature and complete,*
> *not lacking anything.*

"And my trial... well, I haven't told any of you this," she said as she looked around at all of us... "I got laid off my job about two weeks ago."

We all gasped.

Then, she turned to me. "I didn't want to tell you because of all the things you're going through. I didn't want you to worry about me."

"Carly," I said sternly, "that's what friends are for. I need to feel useful, too."

"You're right," she said.

"And the silver lining?" I asked.

Carly paused for a moment. Then, she came out with it and burst into laughter. "I hated that job! Maybe I can find one closer... or with some good-looking young man who's destined to be the love of my life and my husband one day."

We all laughed hysterically as we drank our wine. How could I have been away from Carly for so long? I loved her.

"Not to mention," she said, "that it frees up my time to spend with my best friend when she needs me most."

A tear started to fall from my eye. I couldn't tell if it was for sadness or joy.

"OK, Jenna," Carly said as she looked at Mom. "What's your verse?"

"I bet I can guess," I said.

Mom held up her paper with both hands and began to read as if I did not have a clue. "It is Romans 8:28," Mom said.

And we know that in all things
God works for the good of those who love him,
who have been called according to his purpose.

"My suffering or trial," she said, "except for what my daughter Kristen is going through, is Miss Peacock." She emphasized the last two words. "I'm not sure what the purpose or silver lining might be."

"I know what it could be," I said as I looked at Mom. "The grass is not always greener on the other side… Miss Peacock… *duh.*"

Leigh laughed. "My verse fits right in," she said as she went on to read it from Genesis 50:20 –

You intended to harm me,
but God intended it for good
to accomplish what is now being done,
the saving of many lives.

"What man, or Miss Peacock, meant for evil, God will use it for good," she said. "And my trial, I personally don't really have one right now, but I sure would like to solve the assistant lighthouse keeper's murder mystery. I think the silver lining in the fact that we haven't solved it yet is that I keep in shape hiking all over on the peninsula."

Abby looked puzzled, but she picked up her piece of paper she had set on the table. "I don't know any verses, and I don't have a Bible," she said, "but I do have this poem 'Cancer Is So Limited' by Robert L. Lynn that my great aunt sent me once when I was in the hospital. I keep it by my bedside, and it gives me strength. Basically, it says to me that cancer is not the end-all. I can still be strong, and still have my friends. I can still have love, and hope, and even faith in my life."

We were all quiet. I think none of us knew what to say. After a time, Abby spoke, "I'm counting on it," she said, and we all raised our wine glasses.

That evening, floating down the river, will forever be etched in my mind.

Twenty-One

An hour before the trial was to begin, I was so nauseated that I wasn't sure I could even go. I had just finished another round of chemotherapy and wondered – was I nauseous from the brutal drugs that were poisoning my body or from the thought of the court hearing and having to face Billy Ray? Did it even matter why I was nauseous? Could I make it through the trial without having to literally *run* to the ladies' restroom down the hall to be sick?

Mom and Leigh had taken off work and were going to meet Carly in front of the court house and sit with me and Abby behind the state attorney. Brett was also by my side. Any one of them would have taken my nauseous feelings that day, if they could, and just endured whatever came so that I could feel well and participate in the proceedings as a Williams Rule witness. We met Abby in the hall, her brother by her side, and all walked in together. Billy Ray was already at the front defense table, sitting beside his court appointed free attorney. He turned his head and looked over his right shoulder as we walked in.

"All rise," the bailiff called out. "Judge Kenneth Mills presiding, Franklin County Court is now in session in the case of the State of Florida versus Billy Ray Sorles. You may be seated."

I thought I was going to be sick and was wondering how long I could keep it down. The courtroom was full; probably most people who attended were spectators. I knew Abby and I only had a handful of family and friends who had come to offer their support to us. There may have been a reporter from the Apalachicola Times.

The judge looked over at Mr. Kincaid and gave him a nod, I think to let him know that he could begin with opening arguments. Glancing down at his notes on the table, he slowly rose to his feet. Then, he looked back at us before walking over to face the jurors.

"Good morning, ladies and gentlemen of the jury. I'd like to tell you about a young woman in our community named Abby Connors, a young innocent woman who felt secure in our small community. On the day of the crime you will hear about, a Saturday, Miss Connors awoke to our beautiful weather and the simple life we live here on the *Forgotten Coast*. She and her boyfriend had talked about making plans to get together on the weekend. I'm sure you can visualize it. She awakens to see a beautiful morning outside her kitchen window, the sun streaming in, and decides it's a perfect day to go to the beach."

As Mr. Kincaid talks, he walks very slowly back and forth in front of the jury and then stops and looks directly at individual jury members to make a point. He continued.

"After having a bowl of cereal in the kitchen of the family home she shares with her older brother, Miss Connors puts on her bathing suit and cover-up and slips into her flip flops. She grabs her floppy sun hat, suntan lotion, and a towel and heads out the front door and eagerly across the front porch and down the steps to hop in her car. As she backs out of the drive, she doesn't have a care in the world."

Mr. Kincaid pauses before he goes on.

"Miss Connors made a mistake that day... but not what you think. She made a split-second decision to stop by her boyfriend's house, who at that time was Buddy Lee Sorles, the defendant's younger brother, and invite him to go with her."

Mr. Kincaid paused again.

"But, you see, Buddy Lee wasn't home. His older brother, the defendant, however, was. The mistake that Miss Connors made was being too trusting, too naïve, when Billy Ray Sorles opened the door for her and ushered her into the house. The mistake that Miss Connors made was being too trusting and following Billy Ray to a back bedroom when he asked her to and indicated he wanted to show her something. For you see, when Miss Connors entered the back bedroom, the defendant forcefully sexually assaulted her without warning. Miss Connors fought and screamed, but she was no match for this heavy strong man, and no one heard her scream."

At that point, I could see jury members looking over at Abby, a frail small young woman and then over at Billy Ray, a big heavy man.

"The defense will tell you that yes, Miss Connors and he had sexual relations, but it was consensual. What else could the defendant say when evidence was taken the same day, and we have a forensic DNA expert witness scheduled to testify? Ladies and gentlemen of the jury, I will not ask you to simply believe her word against his word. You will hear from the attending physician who treated Miss Connors at the hospital that day, the law enforcement officer who responded, a forensic DNA expert witness, and another young woman, another victim, who will give similar fact evidence under the Williams Rule of a crime that mimics the one done to Miss Connors, of another crime related to this defendant."

At that, Mr. Kincaid began to close.

"As you hear all the evidence, ladies and gentlemen of the jury, ask yourself – would you be as trusting? Would your sister, or daughter or wife be as trusting? We will show beyond a reasonable doubt that this was a crime of sexual battery thrust upon an unsuspecting young woman who could have been any woman in this community. This crime was not about the victim. This crime was about the defendant, Billy Ray Sorles, and the evidence that I present will demonstrate that he is guilty and punishable under the law."

With a confident and serious nod to the jury, Mr. Kincaid walked back to his table. There were a few moments of quiet, and then the judge addressed the defense attorney for Billy Ray, and he rose and began his opening argument.

"Ladies and gentlemen of the jury, Mr. Kincaid would have you believe that Miss Connors put on her bathing suit, which by the way was a two-piece with nothing more than a scant open cover-up, and went over to her boyfriend's house with nothing more on her mind than a trip to the beach. He would have you believe that it was just a second thought to stop by their home in the woods adjoining Apalachicola National Forest."

I thought I was going to be sick. In fact, I knew it. I whispered to Brett that I needed to go home and asked if he'd mind if I had Mom take me home.

"What about when you're called as a witness?" he quietly asked.

I took a small notepad and pen from my purse and wrote:

Mr. Kincaid,
I must go home.
I'm going to be sick.
May I be a witness another day?

As I tapped his right shoulder and passed the note up to him, I knew I had to leave *now*. Thank the Lord, he looked back and nodded that I could go. As I quietly got up and hurriedly started across to the aisle, I snagged Mom's arm, and she followed me. I rushed to the ladies' restroom, my mom in tow.

When we came back out into the hall, I said, "Mom, I *have* to go home." She didn't question me, and we walked out to her car and headed back to the Cape.

Mom made me tea and toast when we got home. Just being away from the courthouse made my stomach feel better. I wanted to be there to support Abby, but the trial was making me sick. I would do my best as a witness, I thought, but just not today.

"Right, Lucky?" I asked as I noticed him contentedly lying beside us at the table.

He cocked his head and looked at me intently, slowly beginning to wag his tail. Probably he thought I was talking about him. What a simple life he leads, I thought. Let's see, his decisions for the day… Should I stretch out and take a nap or mosey on over to one of my keepers and get my belly rubbed? Decisions, decisions. I patted his head and then went in to lie down.

Mr. Kincaid called after the trial was over for the day. The judge had called a recess till tomorrow morning at nine o'clock. The prosecution could call their last witness then – me.

Abby called, too. I told her how brave she was and reassured her that I was feeling better and would be there tomorrow to testify on the witness stand. Although we both needed this court trial to resolve what had happened, it was much harder than we had thought.

Tomorrow came all too soon. Mr. Kincaid called me as a prosecution witness first thing. His questions were easy. We had rehearsed what I would say more than one time. None of his questions were surprises. I was to look at him and not at Billy Ray, except when I was asked to identify him as the man that sexually assaulted me at Ada's shop that night.

The hard part was when the defense attorney cross-examined me. I was asked about why I didn't report the crime and wasn't I friends with Abby Connors. I tried to be as brave as Abby, my new incredibly courageous friend.

"Miss Parker, isn't it true that you are friends with the prosecution's main witness, Abby Connors?"

"Yes," I replied.

"And, isn't it true that you would do anything for your friend... including this testimony to substantiate her charge of sexual battery against the defendant?"

"What is true," I said, "is that Abby Connors is indeed a friend of mine and would do anything in the world for me... including putting herself through a case like this so that I could find some resolution and peace. What is true, Mr. Preston, is that I was not as brave as Miss Connors to report his crime against me when it happened."

"Miss Parker, just answer the question."

"Yes, Mr. Preston, it is true. I would do anything for her... but lie."

We made it through the morning, and the jury was dismissed to deliberate. We all went over to the Market Street Pizzeria, Abby, Brett, Mom, Leigh, Carly, and I. Abby's brother had to see a man about repairing his net. Mr. Kincaid said that he'd call Mom or Brett's cell if the jury made a speedy decision.

When I slipped into the booth across the table from Abby, she beamed. That smile... what did I ever do to deserve such a friend? I thought. Brett put his arm around me, and I felt so safe. It was over. It was finally over. Now, all we had to do was wait on the jury's verdict.

Carly and I ordered our usual, a large cheese pizza with extra oregano and shared it with Abby and Brett. We all stuck to sweet iced tea in case we were fortunate enough to go back for a jury verdict. Mom and Leigh sat at another booth close by.

Brett had just helped himself to the last slice of pizza when his cell phone went off. It was Mr. Kincaid; the jury was back. They either found it easy to convict or easy to acquit. We would find out very soon.

As we walked back over to the courthouse, we were all very quiet. Abby reached over and squeezed my hand as we crossed the road. Whatever the verdict, we had done what we could.

There was an air of anticipation in the courtroom as everyone waited for about twenty minutes for the judge to enter.

"All rise. Judge Kenneth Mills presiding. Franklin County Court is now in session in the case of the State of Florida versus Billy Ray Sorles. You may be seated."

We all waited for the judge.

"Jury, please rise. Madam Foreman, have you reached a verdict?"

"We have, Your Honor."

The bailiff walked across the courtroom and took a folded piece of paper from a jury member and handed it to the judge. The judge opened it and read it to himself.

"Will the defendant please stand," the judge said.

Both Billy Ray and his attorney stood.

"Madam Foreman, on the charge of sexual battery, a second-degree felony, how do you find?"

"We find the defendant guilty, Your Honor."

"Sentencing will be scheduled for two o'clock tomorrow. Jury, you are dismissed."

You could hear some shuffling in the courtroom. Neither Abby nor I looked at Billy Ray. It was over. The judge wasted no time. He pounded his gavel. "Court adjourned," he said as he quickly got up and disappeared out his private door.

There was now a buzz of talking in the courtroom. Abby and I hugged. Brett hugged me and then Abby. Mom and Leigh and Carly came over and hugged us both.

"Thank you, Mr. Kincaid," I said as he closed his open briefcase.

Looking at both Abby and me, he said, "Congratulations. You both have stopped this man from ever doing this again."

Mr. Kincaid said that we didn't need to be present for the sentencing. Abby and I both decided that we would let God take care of that. We didn't need to be there. We were both trusting God more, not just to do what we might pray for, but trusting in His sovereignty.

We left the courthouse. As I crossed the side street with Brett and Mom and Carly and Leigh and headed down Market to where we had parked in front of the pizzeria, I turned back and waved to Abby who had parked across from the courthouse on the other side. She waved back and smiled.

We began to get in our cars when all of a sudden, *scree.......ch CRASH.*

"What was that?" Mom exclaimed.

We all came around and looked. A car, a black Porsche, had come flying down the bridge into Apalachicola, hit a pedestrian, and then ran into a street light. We heard someone shout, "Call an ambulance!" as we ran over. There, lying in the middle of the road, was Abby.

Twenty-Two

I would like to say that Abby was taken by ambulance to the hospital and recovered, but that would be a lie. They say she died on impact. The Porsche driver was a law student who was driving from New Jersey down to Panama City Beach to meet his friends. When he came across the bridge entering Apalachicola, he had no idea he was entering a small quaint seaside village and that a young woman would be crossing the street from the courthouse, a trusting young woman. A small service was held at Pioneer Methodist Church. I would never forget Abby.

Before I knew it, spring had turned into summer and summer into fall. It was September 11, 2002, and the anniversary of the 9/11 terrorist attack on the Twin Towers and Pentagon was foremost in the news and all around. Documentaries and interviews with survivors were played and replayed on TV. There was a somber atmosphere everywhere you went. As a nation, we were grieving for the loss of someone's family member, someone's mother, someone's father, someone's son or daughter. We were also grieving for our loss of our sense of security as we knew it. There was a heightened awareness that an attack could happen at any time and we could lose our life or that of a friend or family member.

What others didn't know, other than my small circle of close friends and family, was that this was also the anniversary of my terminal cancer prognosis. On 9/11, I had been told that my time was up, that I had six months or less to live. That was now a year ago.

As I watched the specials on TV, curled up at the end of the sofa, I couldn't help but think how blessed I was. So many people had lost their lives on 9/11. They didn't have time to say goodbye to those they loved. They didn't have time to read one last story to their little daughter or stroke the hair of their sleeping son. They couldn't have one last tea with their mother at their favorite tea room and tell her how much they loved her, how much they always would, and that love lasts forever. They didn't have time to work out conflicts with their husband or boyfriend... but I did.

After the anniversary of 9/11, Jacob turned fourteen on September 21st, Briana turned three on September 24th, and I turned thirty-one on October 24th. No one was more amazed than me.

I knew Mom was savoring every cherished moment we were given during my reprieves when the chemotherapy would work for a time. When I was ill, though, I knew she agonized with me and wondered if this was the end. The cycle had gone full circle again. The cancer was now in my bones, my skull, my shoulder, my ribs, my spine, my hip, my leg bone. The doctors at the Cancer Center told me they didn't have any other chemotherapy drugs to try.

"But this is a cancer research hospital," I protested. "There must be an experimental drug I could try."

"You aren't well enough to be a candidate for the experimental trials," Dr. Kerns told me.

I'm not well enough? I thought. But this could save my life!

"Dr. Kerns, I need to live. I need to live for my daughter."

There was nothing more he could say. This nice-looking kind cancer doctor just stood there. This was the business of his day... *but this was my life.* Reality was beginning to sink in. The terminal path I had so repressed was materializing as a possibility right before my eyes.

Still, only God is in control, I thought. Hadn't he just worked it out where I could have my day in court and not have to sit through and endure an entire lengthy court process? Shouldn't I know by now to trust Him? His ways are higher than ours.

The bad thing about cycles with reprieves is that when they eventually circle around, the pain comes back. My pain, especially in my back, was almost unbearable. I could deny it no longer. Dr. Kerns made arrangements for me to enter the Cancer Center hospital for pain management. I was put on a morphine pump while the doctors experimented with what drug combination to send me home with. I was, without a doubt, already on more narcotics than anyone on the Florida panhandle for any disease. The hospice nurse visited me once a week and conferred with the hospice doctor and Dr. Kerns.

As I lay in my hospital bed, it occurred to me all the pivotal points in my daughter's life that I would not be there for. I asked Mom to bring me paper and envelopes so that I could write to Briana and impart my wisdom of the ages to her, wisdom that I had learned the hard way. I wrote letters for her tenth birthday, when she gets her driver's license, her sixteenth birthday, her first heartbreak, her twenty-first birthday, and her wedding day. I wanted her to know how much her mother loves her, even if I cannot be there.

As I was writing, Brett came in the door. He walked over and gently kissed me on the forehead. Then, he sat down in the high-backed chair they always put beside the bed for a visitor to sit in.

He had those faded tight-fitting blue jeans on... guess things never change, and his oxford shirttail fell over his lap. He rubbed his open hands back and forth on the top of his pant legs as if something was on his mind.

"Kris, we have to talk," he said.

"OK," I said as I put my writing materials away by my side and sat up straighter in the bed. "What's up?"

"Kris, whatever happened to our love, the way we were before you left the Cape, our plans? Just because you decided to move, and I don't mean that the way it sounds, my love didn't go away."

I knew all too well that just because you change your geography, love doesn't end. But what could I say?

"Brett, I feel like we're becoming closer every day. Aren't things OK?"

"Kris," he said and then took a deep breath before he continued, "the first day you went with Carly to the state attorney's office at the court house to see about pressing charges against Billy Ray, Carly told me – that day, Kris, she told me – about your stop at Dr. Connelly's office. She told me that you got a DNA test on Briana and told the nurse that a man would be coming in at a different time to be tested."

I sat quietly and listened.

"You know Dr. Connelly has been our family doctor for years, just as he has been yours. Well, after Carly told me that, I went in and told the nurse I was there to have a DNA sample taken for paternity of Bri."

I looked at him dumbfounded. I had forgotten all about that day.

"Kristen, do you even remember when we were together on New Year's Eve… just before you left?" Then, he slightly raised his voice, not enough to disturb other patients in nearby rooms, but enough to make an impact. "You have spent so much of your life, the last three years, running and paying for someone else's sin. The court trial with Billy Ray is over. Kris, it's time for the truth."

Yes, I had remembered being with Brett to celebrate New Year's Eve. It was wonderful. I was almost done with law school and we were beginning to make plans… plans to get married, plans for our future. I also remembered that Brett and I had gotten caught up in a moment of passion that night on the beach, and then we had decided that we wanted to wait to be together until our marriage. What I didn't remember, what had been a blur since the rape just a couple nights later, were the intimate details. It was like *SLAM*, the rape changed everything.

"Kris, Briana looks so much like you that it's hard to see anyone else in her. She's like a miniature you. I've seen pictures of you when you were her age, and it's hard to tell if it's you when you were younger or Briana, the long blonde hair, the blue eyes, and the same face." He paused and was still.

It was true. Briana looked like a little me. Brett, with his sandy colored hair and blue eyes didn't look much different.

"Kris, you didn't need to leave back then. Doesn't the Bible say to cast all your anxiety on God? You had God and, Kris, you had me."

He was right, but at the time I was so traumatized I didn't see it. I allowed someone else's sin to consume my life.

Just then, a young woman came in with a folder at her side. She walked over to where I was sitting up in the hospital bed and Brett in the chair. She didn't say anything but looked over at Brett as if he knew why she was there.

"Kristen," Brett said, this is Sue Ann from the hospital business office. He rose and took the folder and pen from her. "Sue Ann is a notary and I asked her to come up and notarize your signature on this paper authorizing me to pick up the lab test results for you from Dr. Connelly's office." He took the piece of paper out of the folder and handed it over to me as he stood by my bedside.

I was stunned.

Then, he said softly, "Kris, we need to do this."

He was right. It was just that it had been thrust upon me so suddenly. I took the pen and signed my name. Then, Sue Ann stamped it and wrote some things in the small box.

"Thank you, Sue Ann," Brett said.

"You're welcome," she said as she turned and left.

"Kris, I'm going to go down and pick this up before they close. I'll bring the results back, and we can look at it together." He bent over and kissed me again on the forehead.

I was still so stunned, I said nothing. Did I even want to know the results? What if…

It wasn't long before Brett was back, but it seemed like it was forever.

"Kris, it will be OK no matter what it says. I love you, and I'm not going anywhere." He sat beside me on the edge of the bed with a sealed envelope in his hands with the name *Kristen Parker* written on the front. Brett started to hand the envelope to me.

"You open it," I said as I looked at him somewhat apprehensively.

He leaned in beside me and took the envelope in one hand and gently slipped his fingers across it with the other to open it. Then, he took the piece of paper out and looked at it. I could see lab type results and something written, a short sentence or two, on the bottom.

A tear started to fall from Brett's right eye. In a soft voice, he read the last sentence – "It is with 99.9 percent accuracy that the male tested for paternity, Brett Michael Carter, *is* the father of the child tested, Briana May Parker."

Feelings of relief overtook me. All this time…

Brett wrapped his arms around me, and we cried. Tears of relief, tears of sadness for all the time we had wasted, and tears of joy. After what seemed like almost an hour, Brett rose as he took a small box from his jeans' pocket and opened it.

"Kristen Parker, will you marry me?" he asked.

I looked directly into his eyes. "Yes, Brett Carter, yes, I will marry you."

He gently and tenderly slid the ring on my finger. Brett and I both agreed that it looked right at home there… where it was meant to be.

No one seemed surprised when we told them. Most people wondered what took us so long. Mom and Leigh and Carly wasted no time in planning for a wedding. It would be held at Pioneer Methodist, a small service, and Briana, of course, would be the flower girl.

I remained in the hospital a few days till they were able to get my pain under control. The handful of pills I took several times a day could have opened a pharmacy by itself. Thank the Lord I had hospice care that would provide all the costly medications that I needed.

On the morning I was discharged, Mom picked me up, and we went shopping for a wedding dress on the way home. Then, we had tea and sandwiches in our kitchen on the Cape with Lucky underfoot. We talked about our dreams and life and death and men.

"Mom, there's one thing I don't understand about you and Dad, I said. After all he's done… with Viola Peters and not being there at times when you need him most, how can you have any feelings for him whatsoever. It's as if you're living in a black and white world until Dad appears and it turns to color. I don't get it."

"Kristen, my love for your dad doesn't have anything to do with him. It's not based on what he does or doesn't do. It's based on what's inside of me. We're separated for integrity's sake. I couldn't live with a man who didn't treat me the way God intended me to be treated. And the gossip… I was probably the last to know."

"Mom, if Viola Peters has anything to say about it, probably all of Apalachicola knows."

"You're probably right."

It occurred to me then that maybe that's how God's love is for us – not based on what we do or don't do, but on who He is. …and maybe we are the ones who cause the separation from Him. I had to ponder this some more, so I went out to the old bench swing Dad and Jacob had put up under the old oak tree. I stretched out, my head on an old throw pillow at one end. The sun shone through the full branches, and at that moment, I felt that God was truly revealing Himself to me.

Twenty-Three

Love was in the air and excitement was all around. It was in me, so no matter where I went it was there. All I could think of was Brett and our love, the beginning of our life together with Bri, and foremost the wedding. This was a dream I had set aside and never thought would be.

I was dancing around while Mom was working in the kitchen. "Brett and I are getting married," I would say, or "Mom, look at my ring," as I extended my hand, so she could see it only for the thousandth time.

Leigh dropped by to see if there were any last-minute wedding plans to be made. She and Mom were still off work for the summer. In the past, they had often taught summer school, but not this year.

"Girl, we've got to get your mind on something else, so you can make it to the wedding," Leigh said. "You need a distraction. Where's Brett today?"

Mom looked over and answered, "I think he's ordering his tux and coordinating with his family on the wedding plans."

"What about Carly?" Leigh asked.

"Oh, Carly has a new job," I said. "She's working at the Clerk's Office in the Court House."

"Clerk's Office, hmm…" Leigh was in deep contemplation. "I wonder if she could find an address for us on Bow Tucker. His grandfather was a bootlegger back in the 1930's, about the time that the assistant lighthouse keeper on the Cape was murdered. I'd love to see if he had any stories passed down that may give us some clues as to who committed the murder."

"Interesting," I said, although I still couldn't get my mind off my wedding with Brett Hanson, the love of my life. "We could call and ask her."

"Great idea," Leigh said. She was ready to begin investigating the murder again. It had always intrigued her that "someone" had murdered him, and still no one knew who.

I called Carly and before we knew it, she called us back with an address. Bow Tucker lived on the east end of Franklin County off Highway 98 near the Apalachicola National Forest. He didn't have a street address per se, but she had looked at the property records and could take us right to it.

Leigh was delighted. "Ask her what time she gets off work. Let's go tonight," she said with a gleam in her eye.

Carly got off work at five o'clock, was free, and would come out and pick us up. Was a new adventure in the making, I wondered.

Mom was still working in the kitchen making a pot of chili when Carly arrived. "I've got about another twenty minutes to put it all together and then Jacob can watch it," she said. "Why don't you all go down, and I'll meet you there as soon as I can. Where does he live?" she asked as she looked over onto the paper Carly had with directions. Briana was taking a late nap, and Jacob said that he'd watch cartoons with her until we got back.

Leigh and I got in Carly's car, and we headed to the other end of the county. Bow Tucker lived back in the woods with his mother, father, and older sister Tina. It wasn't too hard to find with Carly's directions, but it was way back off the main road.

As we began to pull down the dirt drive, we could see Bow out in the yard about ready to leave in an old bread-type truck. It was beat up and you could tell that it had been repainted many times, this time a rusty red color. We sat there and watched him. He called over his shoulder to his sister that he'd be back as soon as he made the run. Then, he began to close the back doors of the truck and leave but was interrupted. His mother called out to him that he had a telephone call, so he stopped what he was doing and went in the house.

It looked as if Bow wouldn't be available today for an interview about his grandfather and stories that had been passed down… and what was "the run" he was making?

Leigh was in contemplation again. "I'd love to see where he's going," she said. "We could follow him."

Carly looked over at Leigh who was sitting in the passenger seat. "I think he'd see us," she said.

Leigh thought again. "He's in the house. Let's go look in the back of the truck and see what's there." She looked over at Carly and back at me. "Are ya'll game?"

We really didn't have time to think. Carly had pulled her car off the main drive in front of a high firewood pile where it wasn't that noticeable if someone was leaving the house. We all slipped out of the car and crept up to the bread truck to see what was in it.

Leigh went first, of course. She was the adventuresome one. Once she was in, she looked back at us and reported empty crates stacked high. Just then, Bow came out of his house.

"I should be back about seven," he called over his shoulder as he hurried down the front porch steps and across the yard.

Carly and I were so startled, we jumped in the truck. To our dismay, Bow came over, shut the back truck doors, and we heard the latch close.

As soon as we heard Bow get in the driver's seat and the door slam, Carly tried quietly to open the back doors. They were definitely latched. She turned to us. "Looks like we're going along for the ride," she said.

We didn't travel too far, maybe about fifteen or twenty minutes down dirt back roads. I figured we must've entered the National Forest.

We sat on wooden boxes and braced ourselves for the somewhat bumpy ride. When we arrived at his destination, we heard Bow get out of the truck and talk with a couple other men.

Leigh peeked out a crack in one of the back doors.

"What do you see?" I asked.

"It looks like a large flatbed truck with a septic tank on it painted army green... and about a 1950's pickup truck."

"Let me see," I said as I made my way over and peeked through. "You've got to be kidding me!" The men were fastening a copper pipe to the old septic tank and were filling barrels with what looked like a clear liquid. One of the men was about fortyish with lots of facial hair, a red plaid flannel shirt with rolled up sleeves, and denim overalls. It looked like he just stepped out of a movie made in backwoods Tennessee. He had a young boy with him that looked middle school age, his dirty blonde hair curling up around his cap.

I looked over at Leigh and Carly. "I sure hope that was a new septic tank... at least when they started!" Leigh and I could hardly contain our laughter and had to quiet ourselves, so we wouldn't be heard.

"Can I see?" Carly asked and took her turn to look. As soon as she saw what we had seen, she joined in our laughter.

Leigh then took another turn looking out through the crack. "They said something about "apple pie," she said. "They're putting the barrels in the back of the pickup truck and..." she paused, "there's a lot of mason jars with screw off lids that are ready to be loaded somewhere, something about a fake floor in the truck bed."

Just then, Leigh saw Bow approaching the truck. "Quick, hide," she said.

Carly pulled out the back stack of crates, and I slid through. Just then, the doors opened. Leigh and Carly were like deer in headlights. They just stared in their tracks at Bow, and Bow stared right back at them.

"Well, what have we here," he called back to the other men. Another young man we hadn't seen came over. "Dickey, look here."

Leigh and Carly just froze. Then, Leigh spoke up. Bow, we just wanted to see you tonight to ask about your grandfather. We wondered if he had passed on any stories that might give us some clues as to who killed the assistant lighthouse keeper in 1938. It's such an interesting story." She paused as Bow just looked at her. Then she continued, "We saw the doors to your bread truck open when we came to see you, looked in, and just happened to get trapped inside."

"Interesting story…" he grimaced as he motioned for Leigh and Carly to hop down from the truck. He lightly pushed the truck doors back with his right arm.

Once they were down, Dickey looked at Bow and said, "What are we going to do with them? They've seen our operation." Leigh and Carly followed Dickey's gaze as he looked over at their work area. The carport type roof was covered with branches and leaves that most likely couldn't be seen from an airborne small plane or helicopter. What had we gotten ourselves into?

Bow looked at Carly. "Carly Stephens, we've known each other since grade school. I may be runnin' shine, but I'm not no murderer… and neither is my grandaddy. My folks and their folks before them have always run 'shine. It's a way to make a livin'. I've got a route… just like a milkman and make sales in our county for my second cousin," he motioned over to the man in the plaid flannel shirt and overalls, "who brings it down. Now, Carly, what are we going to do with you two?"

I heard Bow say that he had to think about it and motioned the girls over away from the truck. All I could do at that moment was be quiet, very very quiet.

I remembered a verse from the Bible, II Kings 17:39 - "... *Rather, worship the Lord your God; it is He who will deliver you from the hand of all your enemies.*" Right there in the back of the bread truck, I reached out to God. "God, I worship you. You alone are worthy of my praise. I know that I cannot even breathe without you. Please deliver me, deliver us, me, Carly and Leigh, from these enemies." Then, I thanked Him. "Thank you, Heavenly Father, for all your many blessings and for what you are about to do."

I peeked through the narrow opening that had been left when Bow just lightly pushed the bread truck doors shut and saw Carly sitting on a big rock in the clearing near a fire pit. Leigh was standing near her. The man they called Dickey was standing close by with a shotgun. The others continued to load up barrels, gallon jugs, and crates of mason jars wrapped in burlap. I wondered if the bread truck I was hiding in would be next. "Dear God, please deliver us," I prayed again.

It was getting so hot in the truck, and it was nearing the time for me to take more pain medication. I inched closer to the open crack where the back doors were ajar and facing all the action. The very light flow of air felt so good as I breathed it in. I could see that Leigh had noticed me there. She motioned in the direction beside the bread truck where I was and back from it. Then, she slowly and quietly motioned the word "waaait." It was clear she wanted me to wait just a minute, but for what? I stood quietly and just watched.

After about twenty minutes, the man with the shotgun, Dickey, went over to help the others. He leaned the shotgun up against the flatbed truck, and Leigh motioned the word "Go!" as her eyes got big and she threw her arm out and pointed forward. Both she and Carly ran to the side of the bread truck. There was no time to think. I threw open the bread truck doors and raced to meet them. Once I caught up with them, thanks to Carly's outstretched hand and Leigh's keen eye, I could see Mom's car back in the distance behind the tree line. She was in the driver's seat with the car running waiting for us. I learned later that she had gotten to Bow Tucker's just as we decided to be sleuths and hide in his bread truck to see what he was up to. She followed us and waited. Thank the Lord, I thought.

We all made it to Mom's car and piled in as fast as we could. I couldn't believe that I actually made it in my condition, but I did, thank the Lord again. Once we were all in the car, Mom sped away as Bow Tucker and the others had noticed what was happening. Once we were far enough away to know we were safe, we ended the silence, and all broke down and laughed.

Mom drove Carly back to her car, and the rest of us headed back to the Cape. Brett was sitting on the front porch steps holding little Bri when we arrived. It felt so good to be in his arms again, safe and secure.

"What have you girls been up to today?" he asked.

Leigh was the first to answer. "Oh, we've just been trying to distract Kris as she's been so excited about the wedding."

Mom chimed in, "I think we succeeded."

Twenty-Four

The day of our wedding, the weather was gorgeous, and the sun shone bright. Our small church was canopied with sprawling live oaks that were scattered throughout and shaded the property near Mashes Sand. Tables and chairs had been set up for an outside reception after the wedding. The trellis at the entrance was covered in daisies, one of my favorite flowers.

My brother Jacob had put together a small orchestra from his band friends in middle school – one flutist, two saxophone players, and one violinist – to play *Pachelbel's Canon* as the wedding processional began with Briana and Brett's niece Elizabeth, who was ten-years-old, as flower girls. Brett was waiting at the front with our minister, looking ever so proud as he smiled at Briana as she came down the aisle scattering flowers. Johnny was Brett's best man and walked down the aisle with Carly, my maid of honor. Leigh and Brett's younger sister Olivia were bridesmaids.

My dad was not at sea and not at Viola Peters and was there to walk me down the aisle. When it came time, there was a pause in the music, and everyone stood up. *Here Comes the Bride* began to play, and I walked down the aisle on my father's arm. I wore a soft chiffon wedding dress. It was white with the faintest hint of yellow, my favorite color, and a matching veil. My hair had started to grow back in again, and it looked quite stylishly short. I had my granny's lace hanky I carried with my bouquet of daisies – *something old*, my wedding dress was *something new, Mom had loaned me her pearl earrings – something borrowed*, and the baby's breath I had taken from beside Abby's grave in the church yard and put on my veil was *something blue*, maybe not the color, but something blue nonetheless.

Brett was beaming as I walked down the aisle and my dad put my hand in his. We both turned to face the minister.

"Do you, Brett Michael Carter, take this woman to be your lawfully wedded wife, to have and to hold from this day forward, for better or for worse, for richer or for poorer, in sickness and in health, to love, honor, and cherish till death do you part?"

Brett looked deeply into my eyes. "Absolutely," he said. Then, he turned to look at the minister, "I do."

"Do you, Kristen Marie Parker, take this man to be your lawfully wedded husband, to have and to hold from this day forward, for better or for worse, for richer or for poorer, in sickness and in health, to love, honor, and cherish till death do you part?"

"I do," I said beaming.

"At this time," the minister said, "Brett and Kristen have personal vows they would like to give to one another."

Brett turned to face me and held both my hands in his as moisture began to collect on his forehead. He paused as I saw a smile forming in the corner of his mouth, light dancing in his eyes. Then, he began, "From this day forward, I promise to make our time together as one a celebration of life, whether God blesses us with one day or a thousand years. Kristen, my love, my heart has always been with you, and now my body will be as well. I will be your friend and companion during the day to share in your laughter and times of joy. I will be by your side through any hard time and comfort you. At night, I will lay by your side and envelope you with my arms and my love. I give you all that I am, all that I hope to be, all that we are, and all that we hope to be. Kristen, I will love you forever and beyond."

His vows took my breath away. His love filled up my heart, and I have never been happier. Then, I looked at him and began, "Brett, I love you beyond measure and promise to spend all the days I have left on this earth with you. I promise to be your friend and lover, to cherish you and our love all the days of my life. I will walk hand in hand with you on the beach and share all our joys, the greatest joy and gift, our beautiful daughter. In times of sadness, I will hold you in my arms and wipe any tear from your eye. I will love and support you. And, if my body should ever fail, I will hold you in my heart... forever."

There was silence in the church. Then, our minister addressed the congregation and spoke, "Inasmuch as these two have pledged their love and loyalty and lives to one another, God will be with them."

He then turned his eyes on us. "By the power vested in me, I now pronounce you husband and wife." The minister turned to Brett and said, "You may kiss your bride."

Brett lifted my veil, put his arms around me, and kissed me as if he never wanted to let me go. Everyone started clapping, and we released our embrace to face our friends and family. Briana had been sitting with Mom, and she instantly ran toward us, her arms open wide. The three of us walked down the aisle as the music began again.

The reception was wonderful. Jacob's friends moved outside and played their instruments. It reminded me of a tea Mom and I had been to once. The food was wonderful as all the church members had planned and prepared it together. I even had a sense that Abby was there, being we were outside in the church yard and the grave yard was just beyond.

Unbeknownst to me, Brett had arranged for us to go to the Coombs House Bed and Breakfast in Apalachicola the first night of our marriage for our honeymoon. He knew I didn't want to stay away from Briana long, but one night was perfect. Since he was the building inspector, he got the best room in the Inn.

As he carried me over the threshold, I was overtaken by the beauty and charm of the room, the antique furniture and fluffy bed with down comforters. There was a bottle of champagne with glasses awaiting us on a small antique table in the corner, but all we wanted to do was shower and climb into bed and be together. After all this time, we belonged to one another. Tonight, I was not a woman with cancer. Tonight, I was just a woman in love with her husband on her wedding night.

The next day after our breakfast at the Inn, we picked up Briana and went home to begin our new family life together. The beauty of ordinary days… We walked along the shore at sunset and played by the dunes with Briana. The *Forgotten Coast* as it is called… it was ours for the taking, as much ours as savoring a large swig of sweet wine and then slowly swallowing it till it filled us up. As in our youthful days, we would sometimes build a small fire, and Jacob now would come and play his guitar. Brett and I cooked together and enjoyed our young daughter. The joy of ordinary days…

Consider your trials as blessings. If my cancer diagnosis and terminal prognosis hadn't happened, I wouldn't have returned to the Cape, to my mother who is my best friend and to Brett, the love of my life and Briana's father. If my cancer hadn't happened, I may still be a visitor on a stopover in a strange place. I wouldn't have returned to my life. How strange it is that I had to lose my life to find it.

God had used my cancer for my good – Romans 8:28 as Mom would say. My terminal cancer prognosis put me in a position to meet Abby and resolve issues. It took me out of living in the bondage of fear from the rape that happened, and it revealed truths to me – that Briana is our child, Brett's and mine, and that relationships, an extension of God's love, are what's important in life.

God was and is in control… for such a time as this.

Twenty-Five

Some of the best days of my life were yet to be. Brett's love carried over into the days that were unfolding. Married life, and family life with Bri, only enhanced our love. Springtime came, and then summer. I spent countless hours with Briana as she discovered everyday miracles that God has for us all. We picked wildflowers and smelled the beautiful pink mimosa tree puffs that tickled our noses. We pulled petals from a hundred daisies… *He loves me, he loves me not.* We walked barefoot along the bay and discovered treasures, little shells with animals still living inside and delicate baby, mommy, and daddy size horseshoe crab exoskeletons.

Brett never ceased to amaze me with one surprise after another. One summer day, Briana was playing in her sandbox under the shade tree in our yard, and I stretched out on the bright green grass beside her. I was looking up at the clouds pondering life when all of a sudden Brett slipped down beside me.

"Daddy, Daddy," Bri called as she jumped out of the sandbox and ran over to see her dad who had just gotten home from work. He picked her up in the air with a toss, and Briana's giggles abounded. I marveled at how much our lives had changed.

When Briana went back to her play in the sand, Brett and I leisurely lay looking up at the clouds.

"Look, Brett," I said. "There's Granny in the clouds… and an elephant, a whole parade of elephants. They're putting on a play just for us."

"I see," Brett said. He was reminded of how much I had always loved looking up at the clouds and imagining what all the shapes were.

"Kristen, it looks like someone is waving down at us."

"I think you're right, Brett. I wonder who it is," I said as I lifted my arm and waved back.

Such carefree days! We lay there together till the sun began to set, and we could see stars beginning to come out. Then, we took our little girl in the house to get something to eat and ready for bed.

It wasn't more than a couple of days later, a late Saturday afternoon, when Carly showed up at the door announcing that Brett had asked her to babysit.

"Hmm," I responded as I turned and glanced at Brett who had a gleam in his eyes.

"Yes," he said, "I think it's time to go out and see a play designed just for you."

I looked puzzled, remembering our time together just days ago looking up at the clouds. "I'm game. What shall I wear?"

"Probably pants… and bring a sweater in case it gets cool."

I changed from my shorts and tank top and met Brett in the kitchen where Carly had brought out her color cookies for Bri. We kissed our daughter, said goodbye, and off we went.

"So, Brett," I asked when we got in his car. "Where are we going?"

"You'll see," he said as he backed out of the drive.

We drove out on the peninsula to where it makes a turn, the elbow, and pulled in to park in front of a gate.

"Brett, this is the Air Force testing site," I said, looking even more puzzled. We had driven past this small area of land many many times not giving it a second thought. "Brett, what are we doing?"

"You'll see. Follow me," he said as he grabbed an old comforter and picnic basket from the back seat. He walked around the car and opened my car door. "Your play awaits, Madam," he said as he extended his arm.

I smiled and took his hand, wondering what awaited me.

We walked down the fence line and around to the bayside. Brett spread the comforter out and motioned for me to have a seat. He had throw pillows wrapped up in the comforter. He had thought of everything.

It was still daylight, but night was falling.

I opened the picnic basket for a peek and discovered two wine glasses and a bottle of sparkly apple cider. I looked over at Brett.

"I knew you were taking a lot of medications, but we have to celebrate," he said.

"And what are we celebrating?" I asked as I smiled back at him.

"Just being together and... a show in the sky about to unfold designed just for you."

I was puzzled but played along. Inside the picnic basket, there were also sandwiches, antioxidant rich sandwiches, Brett said, with avocado and my favorite cheese. I couldn't imagine when Brett had made them. I didn't even remember having bought the ingredients at the grocery store. Brett must have been undercover.

We ate our sandwiches and drank our sparkly apple cider. Then, I heard a loud noise and looked up. This small piece of land was used by the Air Force for low impact military use. Brett motioned toward two small jets in the sky and told me that a pilot buddy of his clued him in that he and another pilot would be practicing tonight for an air show that would later be at the Air Force Base in Panama City. We lay back on our pillows and marveled at the site. The aerial acrobatics they had mastered were spectacular. No one was around but us. Brett was right. It was a show in the sky just for us, just for me. I had never felt more loved.

Brett bent down and kissed me, a soft lingering kiss. I wished those days would never end.

Twenty-Six

And now... I'm in the intensive care unit at our local hospital. Brett and I had been enjoying this particular Saturday morning, having our coffee together and watching Briana play. It was a perfect morning, when all of a sudden, I could not get my breath. It just wasn't there. It wouldn't come. Brett called for paramedics right away, and the ambulance took me to the closest hospital.

Mom was called and came right away with Jacob. They stayed with me till late in the night while I was still in the emergency room and until I was admitted. Brett had taken Briana home to put her to bed for the night. When I kissed her goodnight and hugged her tight, I didn't want to let her go. Someone, one of Dad's friends, went out in his fishing boat to find him. It could be days before they're back. Would it be in time? I wondered.

That first night, I was moved to intensive critical care. Would Mom know where to come in the morning? Of course, she would. She was resourceful. She would ask and find me. And Brett... he would make it here.

That first morning after I was admitted, I was anxiously anticipating my mother's arrival. The intensive care unit was built around a large nurses' station with wall-less patient rooms on three sides. The curtains that divided us were closed on the sides but drawn in the front, so the nurses could keep a constant eye on all of us.

"Good morning," one cheery nurse said as she entered my room.

"Good morning," I responded and gave her a smile. "My mother's coming up. She should be here any minute." I told her.

The nurse rolled the narrow bedside table out of the way and then took my blood pressure and listened to my chest. "Breakfast will be up soon," she said as she left and walked back to her station about five steps away to make notes in a chart.

I noticed some paper and a pen on the table the nurse had just moved across the room. I could write Briana this morning, I thought. As I slipped off the bed and took a step to cross the room, my lungs were no more. I caught a glimpse of my mother entering the unit across the way, heard "Code Blue" shouted loudly and many feet running toward me. The curtain was closed, and my mother was asked to wait. I would never talk to her again. When the curtain was opened, and she would see me again, I was breathing with a respirator and heavily sedated.

Days passed. Sometimes, when my sedation would begin to wear off, the nurses would give me what seemed like just a few seconds before giving me the next dose. My mother had asked for these few seconds to be allowed to tell me how much she loved me. And once, I had noticed my cousin Rebecca, the cancer doctor in our family, had come to talk with my mom and dad and Brett. I could only surmise the acuteness of my condition. Usually, we would only call Rebecca with minor questions or to ask for her advice when choosing a doctor.

And now, on this my fifth day in the unit, I seem to be coming out of sedation, and through almost closed eyelids I see my dad standing by my bed. With pleading eyes, I reach out to him. My mind is speaking, but no words come out. Love me, love me Dad. It seems I have been trying to catch pieces of you my whole life. You are like a shooting star leaving stardust behind... and I am trying to catch one of the particles. Since I was about fourteen, you've swooped in and out of my life, there for a short time and then off again to find escape in your fishing boat or whatever project you could find. Don't you know what I've learned? Don't you know that everything that's important is right here?

I am able to slowly move my eyes under my barely open eyelids. As I look around my bed from my far left to right, I see Mom, Dad, Johnny, Jacob, Leigh, Carly, and Brett. I know my eyes are just barely open, and they don't know if I am aware of them or not... but I am, and I feel their presence. Even though I am at my death, isn't this what life is about?

Will I ever find out who killed Mr. Marler, the assistant lighthouse keeper? I think I will soon. Maybe I can let you all know when I see you again. You know, I will see you again. *Mom, Leigh, Carly and me, Best friends we'll always be.*

Brett, I will love you forever. Take care of our precious Briana.

Son and Jacob, you are my brothers and will always be. You are in my heart.

Mom, remember... no matter where I am, I am your best friend.

A whiff of sea air from the Cape seems to cross over me, enlightening my senses, and I faintly hear the sound of crashing waves. Am I dreaming? Then...

...Abby? ...*Jesus, is that you?*

I look back. I love you all.

No matter where I am, *I am.* My heart only knows that it loves. And it will do so forever.

Epilogue

I Asked the Lord Why

I don't know why it happened.
I don't know why she died.
I only know I loved her
And on that day I cried
And I asked the Lord... Why?

Why two hearts joined as one
Can never be again?
Why must I give up the gift
Of my daughter and my friend?
And I asked the Lord...Why?

Why do I say a prayer
When it seems it isn't heard?
And why do I still live my life
According to God's word?
Yes, I asked the Lord... Why?

And the Lord answered...

You will see her again.
That, I promise you.
And you both will have a voice again
And a body that's brand new.
And you can ask me then... Why?

Together you will frolic.
You will see her smile again.
And I will be with both of you
Forever till the end.
And you can ask me then... Why?

She has just gone before
On a trip that you will take
And you both shall live forever more
Since I died for your sake.
Yes, you asked your Lord... Why?
Just know I heard your cry.
You will never die.

Granny's Hamburg Stroganoff Recipe
(from Chapter Twelve)

1 can sliced mushrooms drained
1 cup finely chopped onion
1 clove garlic minced
2 tablespoons butter
1 pound ground chuck or sirloin
1 can cream of chicken soup
1 tablespoon flour
1 teaspoon salt
¼ teaspoon pepper
1 cup sour cream
noodles and parsley

Stir mushrooms, onions, and garlic in butter
until onion is almost tender.

Add meat and cook until brown. Remove from heat.

Mix soup, flour, salt & pepper, and stir into meat mixture.

Heat over medium until boiling, stirring constantly.

Lower heat, cover and simmer 10 minutes.

Stir in sour cream and heat through.

Serve over hot cooked noodles. Sprinkle with parsley.

Serve with love.